漢字簡說

漢・英

Chinese Character Briefing

Chinese-English

邢福雷 Ying Fuk Lui 著

邢荃 Idy Ying 修訂

開卷有益

Reading enriches the mind

目 錄

序言

我和作者邢先生是多年的摯友。他 1968 年畢業於北京外國語專科學校，曾經在內地擔任中學英語教師，1978 年定居香港，棄教從商。他既是一位成功的商人，也是一位治學嚴謹、學識淵博的英、漢語言文字學者。

邢先生到港初期曾經擔任過輔導香港 US IBM Education Centre 教員中文的業餘教師。這些外籍教員都是高級知識分子，他們有些人對漢字也有一定程度的了解。有一位教員專門研究漢字的結構，希望從中窺探中國人的思維方式和想像力。當作者對他演繹甲骨文「女」字是「一位行叉手禮的謙卑的女子象形」；「母」字是在「女」字的基礎上加上兩點，這兩點是乳房，表示餵奶；「毋」字是將乳房和私處畫一條線鎖住，表示「禁止，不准姦淫」，他忍俊不禁的説：「Mr. Ying, why not write a book?」（邢先生，為什麼不寫一本書？）這句話點燃了作者寫這本書的熱情的火苗。

文字、語言和文學是我們相當投機的話題。我們有時為了一個字的不同演繹而探討和爭論。比如對「災」字的演繹，我認為「巛」是指水災，而作者卻偏向於「巛」是火燒屋子時露出的「屋脊的殘骸」。我們都像謙謙君子，不但求同存異，而且反過來為對方的演繹查找證據，為的是集思廣益，集腋成裘，寫好這本書。作者常常談到外國友人對漢字的好奇和迷惑。他們提出許許多多的問題，有些問題是已經有了答案的，比如他們説漢字的結構是雜亂無章的，其實不然，「六書」便是歸納了漢字的結構和使用方法的六條例；有些問題是還在爭論而無結果，比如繁體字和簡化字的爭議到底孰是孰非；有些問題是無法解答的謎團，比如為什麼甲骨文發現之前的三千多年中沒有任何文史資料記載，也沒有任何民間傳説，連一點蛛絲馬跡都沒有。作者如實的把這些問題都包含在書中，並且深入淺出的加以述説。作者在寫作過程中，博覽群書，刻苦鑽研，每每產生靈感或是新的觀點都會與我分享，書成之後，邀我作序也就順理成章了。

《漢字簡説》並非是學術性的書籍，而是一本科普的讀物。它沒有堆砌大量的繁瑣枯燥的資料來論證某個專題，而著力用生動形象幽默的文字來簡述漢字的產生和演變過程，讓讀者在輕鬆有趣的閱讀中明瞭漢字的深刻內涵和來龍去脈。

作者將許許多多大大小小的漢字現象和常識，融會貫通，運用巧妙的方法，將複雜的問題簡單化，形象化，分門別類的列舉了二十七個專題，一百八十九條細目，運用通俗易懂的文字，甚至簡簡單單的三言兩語就把各個條目説得清清楚楚。讀者既可以通讀全書，亦可以隨意查閱某條目的講解。

或許有的讀者會問，關於漢字的書已經汗牛充棟，還有必要再寫嗎？我要説，看過此書，你就會明白，不但有必要再寫，而且邢先生還確實寫出了新意。下面略舉本書與眾不同的亮點。

漢字的源頭可以追溯到三千多年前商代晚期的甲骨文，甚至追溯至約五千年前新石器時代的陶文。那麼甲骨文和陶文的源頭又是什麼呢？難道甲骨文和陶文是無源之水，無本之木？對此問題，確無定論。邢先生對此大膽假設，小心求證。他根據古人見鳥獸蹏迒而造書的記載，說明在原始時代，人們已經會在地上畫一些簡單而有意義的圖像。這些圖像可能成為後來陶文和甲骨文的原創意，漢字大概是這樣從無意識到有意識的，經過許多世代的慢慢的創造出來的，這是意料不到的收穫。作者對漢字起源的直觀可說是尋幽入微，他明確而肯定的寫道，五千年前結繩記事中的「結」的意思至今仍然運用在記事的詞語之中，例如「小結、總結、結論、結束、結案」等等，具有極強的說服力，足見邢先生對漢字研究的功力之深厚、表述之象形透徹。

幾千年的中華文明是書之不盡，言之不完的。要闡明某方面的文明，若不是長篇大論，恐怕是很難言盡其意。邢先生在書中常常通過寥寥數字的演繹手法，就言簡意賅的表述和傳達古代文明。例如，他利用一組字：「祖、孝、君、臣、男、女、母、毋、父、夫、妻、兄、弟、姐、妹、子、好、家、人」等各字的結構分析，將中華民族的倫常綱紀演繹得躍然紙上；他通過分析「日、月」兩字的結構來解釋「陰陽」是中國的古代哲學思想；他舉例說明漢字原先用來祭祀神靈，打聽神意，所以漢字能與神鬼溝通，能給人帶來好運，能修身養性，還能治病等等，中國人確實是這樣使用漢字的。

漢字的三個特徵是「形、音、義」。邢先生除了講述漢字的形和義，還著力講述漢字的讀音。他指出，象形文字的讀音是因其「形」而得其「音」。比如形象字「牛」是「牛」這個動物的簡筆圖畫，它的讀音就是讀這個動物的名稱「牛」。他進而說明這就是為什麼可以用不同的方言來讀同一個字，而它的意思不變。這就是為什麼漢字可以成為多方言的中華民族的連接紐帶。這就是為什麼部分漢字能為韓國、日本、越南所借用；作者還將漢字與拉丁文字比較，得出的結論是，部分漢字的單字是可以用任何語言來讀，而拉丁文字只能按照其拼音來讀，這種大膽的嘗試不無道理；作者羅列了漢字的讀音及其注音方法的發展史，對從口頭教授法、直音法、反切、威妥瑪氏拼音、國語注音符號到普通話拼音都做了簡明扼要的講述和比較。他能夠在很小的篇幅裡，條理清楚講述漢字的讀音和注音歷史，是極為難能可貴的。

中國古人創造的文化符號，不僅有文字符號，還有八卦符號和符籙符號。作者明確的強調這三種符號有著密切的關聯，共同承載著遠古時包羅萬象的文化內容。作者在書中順帶介紹八卦符號和符籙符號，對外國讀者進一步了解中國文化尤其能給予極大的啟發和幫助作用。

漢字的命運與中華民族的興衰是緊密的聯結在一起的。在歷史上，漢字曾被交趾（部分交趾今為越南）、韓國（今南、北韓）和日本等借用，因而形成了漢字文化圈。在盛唐時期，許多外國留學生到中國來學習文化。當時，日本的上層社會紛紛仿效中國人，並認為懂得書寫漢字才算是有教養的人。今天，中國的經濟文化的發展影響整個世界，漢語熱席捲全球，漢字的傳播更加廣泛。向世界推廣漢字，推廣中華文化，也是邢先生撰寫本書的主要目的。

《漢字簡説》是一本讀來有趣，能增進漢字知識的書。也是一本學習中文和英語的很好的參考書。值得大力推介，值得讀者好好閱讀。

楊海英

楊海英
香港著名小說作家
著有《碟血情仇錄》、《無韻的古歌》等多部長篇和中篇歷史小說，並於2020年獲「首屆香港文化名人成就評選活動」頒予「歷史小說終身傑出成就獎」。現為香港文化藝術界聯會副主席、香港文化促進協會副會長、香港文化發展研究會永遠榮譽會長和《香港書評家》雜誌副會長。

Preface

Mr. Ying, my best friend for many years, graduated from Peking College of Foreign Languages in 1968. He then worked as a middle school English teacher in China before settling in Hong Kong in 1978, where he left teaching to pursue a career in business.

He once served as a part-time Chinese tutor at the Hong Kong American IBM Education Centre. While teaching, he explained that the Chinese oracle bone script （女 , girl） represents a polite girl. By adding two dots to , it becomes（母 , mother） , where the dots symbolize a mother's breasts. Further, by drawing a line across the breasts and private parts, it forms （毋 , never） , conveying the meaning "never sexually harass a mother". Upon hearing this explanation, a teacher at the Centre couldn't help but say, "Mr. Ying, why not write a book? " This remark sparked Mr. Ying's passion for writing this book.

Some foreign learners are curious about Chinese characters, as their structures may seem disordered. However, Chinese characters are systematically categorized into the "Six Writing Forms", known as liushu（六書） . The debate over complex and simplified characters is unlikely to be resolved anytime soon.

Interestingly, although oracle bone scripts were discovered more than three thousand years later, no historical documents or even folklore had ever mentioned them throughout those millennia. This remains an unsolved mystery. Mr. Ying briefly explores these topics in his book.

Bookstores are already filled with books on Chinese characters, so is another one really necessary? I would say yes—Mr. Ying offers fresh perspectives and intriguing interpretations that make this book well worth reading.

Mr. Ying distills the fundamentals of Chinese characters into twenty-seven chapters, covering 189 key points. Readers can either explore the entire book or selectively read the points that interest them.

To this day, the origins of oracle bone script and pottery inscriptions remain unknown. Based on ancient historical texts, Mr. Ying believes that the ancestors' drawings on soil were the earliest forms of writing—ephemeral creations that could not have survived to the present day.

Mr. Ying introduces the ancient Chinese philosophy of Yin and Yang by analyzing the characters 日（"sun"）and 月（"moon"）. He also traces the origins of record-keeping back 5,000 years, demonstrating how ancient people used knots to store information—an idea reflected in modern Chinese terms such as 小結（small knot）meaning "brief summary", 總結（total knots）meaning “summing up”, 結論（knot comment）meaning “conclusion”, 結束（knots tied up）meaning “end”, and 了結（finalized knot）meaning “settled”.

Furthermore, he vividly explains the moral and ethical principles of Chinese culture through a set of characters, including 祖（“ancestor”）, 君（“monarch”）, 臣（“official”）, 男（“man”）, 女（“woman”）, 母（“mother”）, 毋（“never”）, 父（“father”）, 夫（“husband”）, 妻（“wife”）, 兄（“elder brother”）, 弟（“younger brother”）, 姐（“elder sister”）, 妹（“younger sister”）, 子（“child”）, 好（“good”）, 家（“home, family”）, and 人（“people”）. Mr. Ying’s interpretations are both concise and compelling.

Mr. Ying explains that Chinese characters can be compared to international traffic signs, used to communicate with spirits, promote personal well-being, bring good fortune, and even heal illnesses. The Chinese people have long embraced these uses in their culture. Don’t you think that’s amazing?

Besides the form and meaning of Chinese characters, Mr. Ying also emphasizes their pronunciation. The pronunciation of a character is derived from the name given to the object it represents in pictographic form. This explains why Chinese characters can be read in different dialects and why they were historically borrowed by Korean, Japanese, and Vietnamese languages. To help readers understand the evolution of phonetic notation, Mr. Ying provides a comprehensive list of phonetic symbols used throughout history.

To help foreign readers gain a deeper understanding of Chinese culture, Mr. Ying briefly introduces the ancient Chinese semiotics of Ba Gua（八卦）, also known as “the Eight Trigrams”, and Fu Lu（符籙）, “Taoist Magic Figures”. These concepts may spark curiosity among foreign readers.

Through this book, readers will also discover many fascinating stories about Chinese characters, making their learning experience both insightful and enjoyable.

Yang Hai Ying

簡介

華夏歷史，上下五千年，而漢字是中華文化的基本元素。要深入體會古今中華之文明，就必須了解漢字。

本書是作者應其外國朋友的要求而寫的，故以中英文對照編寫，除了能讓中文讀者閱讀，同時為了讓英文讀者在掌握一些基本的漢語和漢字知識之餘，在閱讀本書的中文部分，也許可以領略到漢字的豐富的想像力。

每一個漢字都是一幅美麗的圖畫，一個古老的故事。漢字的歷史悠久，積累了大量的故事。對一些字有不同的演繹，比如金文災（災）字，有一說法巛（巛）是「水」災；另一說法，巛（巛）是火燒屋子時露出的「屋脊的殘骸」。您認為哪種說法合理呢？長篇累牘的演繹漢字，容易使人產生「漢字恐懼症」。我們不可能，也不必要對每個漢字都解說它的起源和演變，但是應該了解這方面的基本知識。有鑑於此，本冊子用隻言片語通俗地介紹漢字的概況，讓讀者輕易了解和學習漢字。

漢字是無法精確翻譯成外文的，例如，「馬」英語譯成horse，「虎」是tiger，但是「馬馬虎虎」就不是horse horse tiger tiger，而是so-so。這類例子並不少。這本書將告訴您為何有這種漢字現象。

您會相信嗎，漢字能跟國際交通標誌比較，能與神鬼溝通，能修身養性，能給您帶來好運，還能治病等等，這並非匪夷所思，中國人是這樣使用漢字的。

漢字的形、音、義在幾千年的中華文化發展過程中，發生過異變、碰撞、增減、繁簡、錘煉，例如「姐」字，原來蜀謂之「母」，而淮南謂之「社」，後來變成「姊」的意思。從不同角度演繹漢字，就會產生不同觀點，是在所難免的。作者希望《漢字簡說》能起到抛磚引玉的作用。

邢福雷

Introduction

The history of Chinese civilization spans over five thousand years, with Chinese characters serving as a foundational element of Chinese culture. To truly understand the civilization of China, both ancient and modern, one must first understand Chinese characters.

This book was written at the request of the author's foreign friends and is presented in a bilingual Chinese-English format. This approach enables Chinese readers to enjoy the content while allowing English readers to grasp the basics of Chinese language and characters. Through learning Chinese characters, readers can also appreciate their rich imaginative qualities.

Each Chinese character is a beautiful picture, an ancient story in itself. With a long history, Chinese characters have accumulated numerous stories. Sometimes a character can have different interpretations. Consider the bronze script 災（災 zāi, ㄗㄞ）, "disaster". The part 巛（巛）has been interpreted as either "flood", or as representing the "remains of a rooftop after a fire". Which interpretation seems more plausible? Complex interpretations of characters can lead to "character phobia". While it is neither possible nor necessary to explain the origin and evolution of every character, some fundamental knowledge is essential. Hence, this booklet provides a brief and accessible introduction to the essence of Chinese characters, allowing readers to learn and understand them with ease.

Every language has its own peculiarities, where there is no perfect translation. The original meanings of Chinese characters are often lost in translation. For example, 馬（mǎ, ㄇㄚˇ） translates to "horse" and 虎（hǔ ㄏㄨˇ） to "tiger", but the idiom 馬馬虎虎 does not translate to"horse horse tiger tiger"; instead, it means "so-so". Examples like this are not uncommon. This book will explain why such linguistic phenomena exist in Chinese characters.

Would you believe that Chinese characters can be compared to international traffic signs, communicate with spirits, promote personal well-being, bring good fortune, and even heal illnesses? This is not a far-fetched idea; Chinese people have indeed used characters in these ways.

Over thousands of years of Chinese cultural development, the forms, sounds, and meanings of characters have undergone changes, simplifications, and refinements. For example, the character 姐（jiě, ㄐㄧㄝˇ）originally referred to "mother" in the Sichuan region, but "Temple of the Land Deity" in Huainan, and eventually evolved to mean "older sister". Interpreting Chinese characters from different perspectives naturally leads to various viewpoints. The author hopes that Chinese Character Briefing will attract ideas and receive responses from readers.

Ying Fuk Lui

一　漢字
Han Zi

1

一般而言，中國文字是指漢字，
具體的說，是漢族的語言文字。

「國語」是指在清末民初（1911 年左右）時期，為國民共同使用，具有明確規範的漢族語言的口語。

「普通話」是指中華人民共和國推行，國家通用語言文字法所規定，現代標準的漢族語言的口語。

「華語」是海外華人對漢語的泛稱。

有一些漢字的「國語」讀音和「普通話」讀音是有差異的，例如，「垃圾」的台灣國語讀音是ㄌㄜˋ ㄙㄜˋ，lè sè，普通話的讀音是ㄌㄚ ㄐㄧ，lā jī，「淆」的國語讀音是ㄧㄠˊ，yáo，普通話的讀音是ㄒㄧㄠˊ，xiáo。

「國語」、「普通話」和「華語」所指是一樣的，比如普通話的歌曲和普通話的影片都分別叫做「國語歌曲」和「國語影片」，或者叫做「華語歌曲」和「華語影片」。

Chinese characters generally refer to Han characters (Han Zi), specifically the scripts of the Han ethnic group.

國語（guó yǔ, ㄍㄨㄛˊ ㄩˇ）, "Mandarin", refers to the standardized spoken language of the Han ethnic group that was commonly used by the public during the late Qing dynasty and early Republic of China（around 1911）.

普通話（pǔ tōng huà, ㄆㄨˇ ㄊㄨㄥ ㄏㄨㄚˋ）, "Putonghua", refers to the modern standard spoken language of the Han ethnic group as specified in the language laws promoted by the People's Republic of China.

華語（há yǔ, ㄏㄨㄚˊㄩˇ）, "Hua Yu", is a general term used by overseas Chinese communities to refer to the Chinese language.

There are some differences in pronunciation between Mandarin and Putonghua for certain Chinese characters. For example, the pronunciation of 垃圾 , "garbage", in Taiwan Mandarin is ㄌㄜˋ ㄙㄜˋ（lè sè）, while in Putonghua it is ㄌㄚ ㄐㄧ（lā jī）. The pronunciation of 淆 , "confuse", in Mandarin is ㄧㄠˊ（yáo）, while in Putonghua it is ㄒㄧㄠˊ（xiáo）.

The terms "Mandarin", "Putonghua", and "Hua Yu" refer to the same concept. For instance, songs and films in Putonghua are referred to as "Mandarin songs and films", or "Hua Yu songs and films".

2

中國有五十六個民族，十四億人口。

There are 56 ethnic groups in China, boasting a total population of 1.4 billion.

民族	注音	標準羅馬字母拼寫
Ethnic groups	注音符號 Pinyin Mandarin Phonetic Symbols	Standard Latin Alphabet Spelling
漢族	Hàn Zú ㄏㄢˋ ㄗㄨˊ	Han
蒙古族	Měnggǔ Zú ㄇㄥˇㄍㄨˇ ㄗㄨˊ	Mongol
回族	Huí Zú ㄏㄨㄟˊ ㄗㄨˊ	Hui
藏族	Zàng Zú ㄗㄤˋ ㄗㄨˊ	Tibetan
維吾爾族	Wéiwúěr Zú ㄨㄟˊㄨˊㄦˇ ㄗㄨˊ	Uyghur
苗族	Miáo Zú ㄇㄧㄠˊㄗㄨˊ	Miao
彝族	Yí Zú ㄧˊ ㄗㄨˊ	Yi

民族	注音	標準羅馬字母拼寫
壯族	Zhuàng Zú	Zhuang
	ㄓㄨㄤˋ ㄗㄨˊ	
布依族	Bùyī Zú	Bouyei
	ㄅㄨˋㄧ ㄗㄨˊ	
朝鮮族	Cháoxiǎn Zú	Choson
	ㄔㄠˊㄒㄧㄢˇ ㄗㄨˊ	
滿族	Mǎn Zú	Manchu
	ㄇㄢˇ ㄗㄨˊ	
侗族	Dòng Zú	Dong
	ㄉㄨㄥˋ ㄗㄨˊ	
瑤族	Yáo Zú	Yao
	ㄧㄠˊ ㄗㄨˊ	
白族	Bái Zú	Bai
	ㄅㄞˊ ㄗㄨˊ	
土家族	Tǔjiā Zú	Tujia
	ㄊㄨˇㄐㄧㄚ ㄗㄨˊ	
哈尼族	Hāní Zú	Hani
	ㄏㄚㄋㄧˊ ㄗㄨˊ	
哈薩克族	Hāsàkè Zú	Kazakh
	ㄏㄚㄙㄚˋㄎㄜˋ ㄗㄨˊ	
傣族	Dǎi Zú	Dai
	ㄉㄞˇ ㄗㄨˊ	
黎族	Lí Zú	Li
	ㄌㄧˊ ㄗㄨˊ	

民族	注音	標準羅馬字母拼寫
傈僳族	Lìsù Zú	Lisu
	ㄌㄧˋㄙㄨˋ ㄗㄨˊ	
佤族	Wǎ Zú	Wa
	ㄨㄚˇ ㄗㄨˊ	
畲族	Shē Zú	She
	ㄕㄜ ㄗㄨˊ	
拉祜族	Lāhù Zú	Lahu
	ㄌㄚ ㄏㄨˋ ㄗㄨˊ	
水族	Shuǐ Zú	Shui
	ㄕㄨㄟˇ ㄗㄨˊ	
東鄉族	Dōngxiāng Zú	Dongxiang
	ㄉㄨㄥ ㄒㄧㄤ ㄗㄨˊ	
納西族	Nàxī Zú	Naxi
	ㄋㄚˋ ㄒㄧ ㄗㄨˊ	
景頗族	Jǐngpō Zú	Jingpo
	ㄐㄧㄥˇ ㄆㄛ ㄗㄨˊ	
柯爾克孜族	Kēěrkèzī Zú	Kyrgyz
	ㄎㄜ ㄦˇ ㄎㄜˋㄗ ㄗㄨˊ	
土族	Tǔ Zú	Tu
	ㄊㄨˇ ㄗㄨˊ	
達斡爾族	Dáwòěr Zú	Daur
	ㄉㄚˊㄨㄛˋㄦˇ ㄗㄨˊ	

民族	注音	標準羅馬字母拼寫
仫佬族	Mùlǎo Zú ㄇㄨˋㄌㄠˇ ㄗㄨˊ	Mulao
羌族	Qiāng Zú ㄑㄧㄤ ㄗㄨˊ	Qiang
布朗族	Bùlǎng Zú ㄅㄨˋ ㄌㄤˊㄗㄨˊ	Blang
撒拉族	Sālā Zú ㄙㄚㄌㄚ ㄗㄨˊ	Salar
毛南族	Máonán Zú ㄇㄠˊㄋㄢˊㄗㄨˊ	Maonan
仡佬族	Gēlǎo Zú ㄍㄜㄌㄠˇ ㄗㄨˊ	Gelao
錫伯族	Xībó Zú ㄒㄧㄅㄛˊㄗㄨˊ	Xibe
阿昌族	Ãchāng Zú ㄚㄔㄤ ㄗㄨˊ	Achang
普米族	Pǔmǐ Zú ㄆㄨˇㄇㄧˇ ㄗㄨˊ	Pumi
塔吉克族	Tǎjíkè Zú ㄊㄚˇㄐㄧˊㄎㄜˋㄗㄨˊ	Tajik
怒族	Nù Zú ㄋㄨˋ ㄗㄨˊ	Nu

民族	注音	標準羅馬字母拼寫
烏茲別克族	Wūzībiékè Zú ㄨㄗㄅㄧㄝˊㄎㄜˋㄗㄨˊ	Uzbek
俄羅斯族	Éluósī Zú ㄜˊㄌㄨㄛˊㄙ ㄗㄨˊ	Russian
鄂溫克族	Èwēnkè Zú ㄜˋㄨㄣㄎㄜˋ ㄗㄨˊ	Evenki
德昂族	Déáng Zú ㄉㄜˊㄤˊㄗㄨˊ	De’ang
保安族	Bǎoān Zú ㄅㄠˇ ㄢ ㄗㄨ	Bao’an
裕固族	Yùgù Zú ㄩˋㄍㄨˋ ㄗㄨˊ	Yughur
京族	Jīng Zú ㄐㄧㄥ ㄗㄨˊ	Jing
塔塔爾族	Tǎtǎěr Zú ㄊㄚˇㄊㄚˇㄦˇㄗㄨˊ	Tatar
獨龍族	Dúlóng Zú ㄉㄨˊㄌㄨㄥˊㄗㄨˊ	Derung
鄂倫春族	Èlúnchūn Zú ㄜˋㄌㄨㄣˊㄔㄨㄣ ㄗㄨˊ	Oroqen
赫哲族	Hèzhé Zú ㄏㄜˋㄓㄜˊㄗㄨˊ	Hezhe

民族	注音	標準羅馬字母拼寫
門巴族	Ménbā Zú ㄇㄣˊㄅㄚ ㄗㄨˊ	Menba
珞巴族	Luòbā Zú ㄌㄨㄛˋㄅㄚ ㄗㄨˊ	Lhoba
基諾族	Jīnuò Zú ㄐㄧㄋㄨㄛˋ ㄗㄨˊ	Jino
高山族	Gāoshān Zú ㄍㄠㄕㄢ ㄗㄨˊ	Gaoshan

3

除了漢字，還有大約三十種不同民族的文字。

Besides Han Zi, there are about thirty different scripts from other ethnic groups.

漢族佔全國人口的百分之九十以上，是有五千多年文明史的中國的主體民族。

The Han ethnic group accounts for more than ninety percent of the national population and is the main ethnic group of China, which boasts a 5000-year history of civilization.

4

龍 (lóng, ㄌㄨㄥˊ)

dragon

		龍	龍	龍	龙
甲骨文	金文	篆書	隸書	楷書	簡體字
Oracle bone	Bronze	Seal	Clerical	Regular	Simple
script	script	script	script	script	form

中國人自稱為龍的傳人。

為什麼中國人喜歡龍？

上天造物要使生態平衡，於是給一些動物長利角，就不再給其長利牙，如牛、犀牛、鹿等等；給一些動物長利牙，就不再給其長利角，如老虎、獅子、犬等等；給一些動物長翅膀，就不再給其長跑得快的腿，如鳥類；給一些動物長跑得快的腿，就不再給其長翅膀，如馬。

中國人要把動物的所有優點集於一身，他們所造的龍，有鹿角，有虎牙，有鳳爪，有蛇身，有魚尾，能飛天，能潛海，無所不能。

The Chinese refer to themselves as "descendants of the dragon".

Why do the Chinese like dragons?

Heaven and nature created to maintain ecological balance. Some animals were given horns but not tusks, like cows, rhinos, and deer; some animals were granted tusks but not horns, like tigers, lions, and dogs; some animals were blessed with wings but not fast legs, like birds; and some animals were endowed with fast legs but not wings, like horses.

The Chinese want to gather all the advantages of animals into one, so they created the image of the dragon with deer antlers, tiger teeth, phoenix claws, a snake body, and a fish tail. It can fly in the sky and swim in the sea, capable of doing anything.

5

叶公好龍（**shè gōng hào lóng,** ㄕㄜˋㄍㄨㄥ ㄏㄠˋ ㄌㄨㄥˊ）

She Gong who loves dragons

中國人是一個幽默的民族。

「叶公好龍」是一個典故。從前，有一個叫叶（讀「攝」音）公的人，他很喜歡龍，在他家的牆壁上和柱子上都畫滿了龍。有一條真龍受到感動而來看望他。當龍來到的時候，可把叶公嚇得要命。這個典故調侃那些既愛龍又怕龍的龍的傳人。

The Chinese is a humorous nation.

叶公好龍

（shè gōng hào lóng, ㄕㄜˋ ㄍㄨㄥ ㄏㄠˋ ㄌㄨㄥˊ）“She Gong who loves dragons” is a well-known allusion. Once, there was a man named She Gong who really liked dragons. His walls and pillars were covered with dragon paintings. Moved by his passion, a real dragon came to visit him one day. However, when the dragon arrived, it gave She Gong a good fright. This allusion mocks those“descendants of the dragons” who both love and fear dragons.

二 文字的起源

The Origins of Chinese Characters

6

結繩記事 jié shéng jì shì

(ㄐㄧㄝˊ ㄕㄥˊ ㄐㄧˋ ㄕˋ)

Keeping records by knotting

五千年前，古人結繩記事，以結為約。

Five thousand years ago, the ancient people recorded events by knotting cords, using knots as agreements.

7

小事小結，大事大結，完事結束。

Small knots represented minor matters.

Big knots represented major matters.

When the matters were solved, the knots were tied up and put aside.

五千年前結繩記事中的「結」的意思，至今仍然運用在記事的詞語之中。

The meaning of 結（jié, ㄐㄧㄝˊ）, "knot" in knotting to record events from five thousand years ago, is still applied in terms related to recording events today.

現代詞語	直譯英語	英語語義
拼音	Word-for-word English translation	Meaning in English
國語注音符號 Modern Chinese terms		
Pinyin		
Mandarin Phonetic Symbols		

現代詞語	直譯英語	英語語義
小結 xiǎo jié ㄒㄧㄠˇㄐㄧㄝˊ	small knot	brief summary
總結 zǒng jié ㄗㄨㄥˇ ㄐㄧㄝˊ	total knots	summing up
結論 jié lùn ㄐㄧㄝˊㄌㄨㄣˋ	knot comment	conclusion
結束 jié shù ㄐㄧㄝˊㄕㄨˋ	knots tied up	end
了結 liǎo jié ㄌㄧㄠˇㄐㄧㄝˊ	finalized knot	settled

8

事情太多太亂了，記不住。

As matters became more and more complicated, people soon forgot what the knots represented.

當事情越來越多和越來越複雜，結繩難以記事的時候，古人使用另一種記事方法，文字由此產生。

Eventually the knots failed to effectively record the increasingly complicated matters. The ancients needed to find a better method to record events, which led to the emergence of characters.

三 什麼是文字？

What does 文字 (wén zì, ㄨㄣˊ ㄗˋ) "Chinese Character" mean?

9

燕 **(yàn, 一ㄢˋ)**

Swallow

甲骨文	金文	篆書	隸書	楷書
Oracle bone script	Bronze script	Seal script	Clerical script	Regular script

古人造字是從描摹實物的形狀開始的。

The ancient Chinese created scripts starting from depicting the shapes of objects.

10

「文字」簡稱為「字」。但是，許多人並不曉得「文」和「字」是兩種不同形狀的字，是有所區別的。

The term 文字（wén zì, ㄨㄣˊㄗˋ）, "script", is often abbreviated to 字（zì, ㄗˋ）, "character". However, many people do not realize that 文 and 字 are two different categories of characters and are distinct.

11

什麼是「文」?「文」即是「紋」，是描摹物象的交錯的線紋，好像一個人胸上的刺青。由於一個「文」表現一個物象，所以「文」是單體圖像。

What is 文（wén, ㄨㄣˊ）? 文 means 紋（wén, ㄨㄣˊ）, which refers to the interwoven lines that depict the shapes of objects, similar to a tattoo on a person's chest. Since a 文 represents a single object, it is a single-object graphic character.

文 (wén, ㄨㄣˊ)

Character

文	文	文	文	文
甲骨文	金文	篆書	隸書	楷書
Oracle bone script	Bronze script	Seal script	Clerical script	Regular script

「文」的甲骨文文，一個胸上有刺青的人，是單體圖像。

The oracle bone script 文 for 文（wén, ㄨㄣˊ）depicts a person with a tattoo on his chest, representing a single image. It is thus a single-object graphic character.

鳥（niǎo, ㄋㄧㄠˇ）

Bird

			鳥	鳥	鸟
甲骨文	金文	篆書	隸書	楷書	簡體字
Oracle bone script	Bronze script	Seal script	Clerical script	Regular script	Simple form

鳥是描畫的交錯的線紋，是一個單體圖像，所以它是一個「文」。

The script 鳥（niǎo, ㄋㄧㄠˇ）, "bird", depicts the interwoven lines of a bird representing a single image. Thus, it belongs to the category of 文（wén, ㄨㄣˊ）, "single-object graphic characters".

木 (**mù**, ㄇㄨˋ)

wood, tree

甲骨文	金文	篆書	隸書	楷書
Oracle bone script	Bronze script	Seal script	Clerical script	Regular script

木是描畫 的交錯的線紋，是一個單體圖像，所以它是一個「文」。

木 The script （mù, ㄇㄨˋ）, "wood" or "tree", depicts the interwoven lines of a tree , representing a single image. Thus, it belongs to the category of 文（wén, ㄨㄣˊ）, "single-object graphic characters".

12

什麼「字」?「字」是「文」之「子」，所以「字」中有一個「子」。「字」是由「文」衍生而來的。「字」含有兩個或以上個圖像，是複合圖像，這是與單體圖像的「文」不同的地方。

What is 字（zì, ㄗˋ）? 字 is analogous to the "baby" of 文 , that is why 字 contains the character 子（zǐ, ㄗˇ）, "baby". 字 is derived from 文 by combining two or more images and is a composite image, which distinguishes it from the single image represented by 文 .

Thus, 字 is the category of <u>compound-object graphic characters</u>, as opposed to 文 , the category of <u>single-object graphic characters</u>.

字（**zì,** ㄗˋ）

character

(無) (none)			字	字
甲骨文	金文	篆書	隸書	楷書
Oracle bone script	Bronze script	Seal script	Clerical script	Regular Writing

字是在 文 的<u>單體圖像</u>上加上一個或多個圖像，創造出新的意思，它是<u>複合圖像</u>，例如字有兩個圖像宀「屋」和子，比喻在屋內產子，形容字的產生方法。

字（zì, ㄗˋ）, <u>compound-object graphic characters</u>, created by adding one or more images to 文（wén, ㄨㄣˊ）, <u>single-object</u>

graphic characters, resulting in a new meaning.

It is interesting to note that 字 is in its very self a compound-object graphic character, formed by combining 宀, "house", and 子（zǐ, ㄗˇ）, "baby", analogous to a baby being born in a house.

古人將「文」與「字」作了人格化的比喻，「文」是母體，「字」是子。《說文解字》說：「字，乳也，子在下」，又說「字者，言孳乳而浸多」。即是說，「字」是由「文」不斷地繁衍出來的許多個「嬰兒」。

The ancient scholars personified 文（wén, ㄨㄣˊ）and 字（zì, ㄗˋ）, with 文 as the mother and 字 as the baby.

Shuowen Jiezi says, " 字 symbolizes nurturing; the baby is below", and " 字 refers to the idea of proliferating and growing gradually". Just like a "mother" giving birth to more and more "babies", many 字, "compound-object graphic characters", are developed from 文, "single-object graphic characters".

13

「文」是如何孳乳（哺乳、繁衍）出許多個「字」？

How does 文（wén, ㄨㄣˊ）, a "single-object graphic character", give birth to so many 字（zì, ㄗˋ）, "compound-object graphic characters"?

鳥是一個「文」。

鳥（**niǎo, ㄋㄧㄠˇ**）**, "bird", is a** 文（**wén, ㄨㄣˊ**）**,**

"<u>single-object graphic character</u>".

在鳥的<u>單體圖像</u>上加上一個或多個圖像或偏旁，創造出新的意思，孳乳（繁衍）出許多個<u>複合圖像</u>的「字」。

By adding one or more graphics or radicals to the <u>single-object graphic character</u> 鳥, many 字, <u>compound-object praphic characters</u>, with new meanings are born.

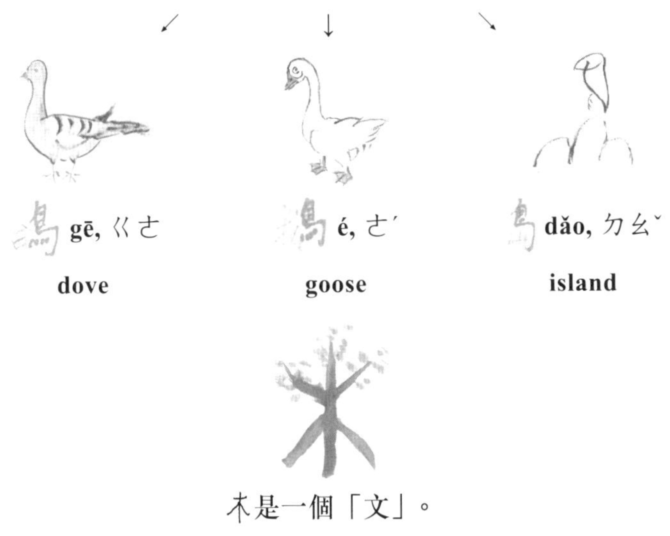

木是一個「文」。

木（**mù, ㄇㄨˋ**），**"wood"，is a** 文，

"<u>single-object graphic character</u>".

在 木 的單體圖像上加上一個或多個圖像或偏旁，創造出新的意思，孳乳（繁衍）出許多個複合圖像的「字」。

By adding one or more graphics or radicals to the “single-object graphic character” 木 , many 字 , compound-object praphic characters, with new meanings are born.

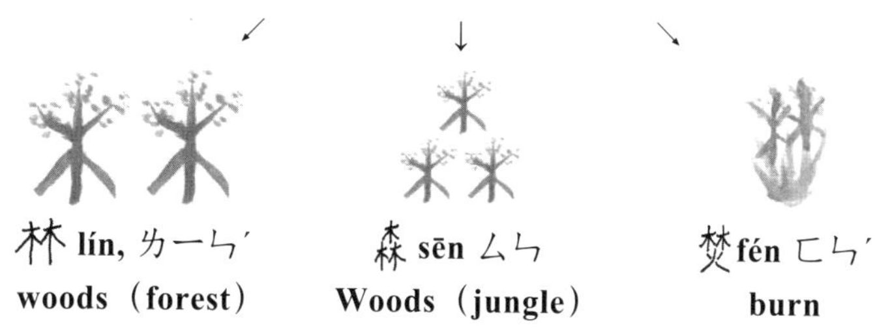

14

文字的產生過程

The Process of the Creation of Chinese Characters

文字不是閉門造車的造出來的，所以沒有文字產生的時間節點。我們相信，在原始時代，人們已經會在地上畫一些簡單

的有意義的圖像，這些圖像是容易消失，不能遺留下來的。人們不斷地創造這樣的圖像和漸漸積累了豐富的經驗。這些經驗極大可能成為後來創造陶文和甲骨文的原創意。要不然，陶文和甲骨文就好像無源之水、無本之木。所以考古學家們總是糾纏不清文字何時開始。

Chinese characters were not invented behind closed doors, so there is no definitive starting point for their creation. It is believed that, in prehistoric times, people were already drawing simple, meaningful graphics on soil - images that would easily disappear and leave no trace. People continued to create such graphics, gradually accumulating experiences. These early experiences very likely inspired the later creation of pottery inscriptions and oracle bone scripts. Otherwise, pottery inscriptions and oracle bone scripts would be a mystery case without clues. This is why archaeologists are constantly debating the exact starting point of Chinese characters.

古人畫圖像表示某種意思，當時沒有意識到他們是在創造文字。例如 的圖像是「魚」的意思，圖像的名稱（yú, ㄩˊ）（注：當時是沒有注音符號的）代表讀音。同時不斷地創造出新的圖像，如在 （魚）的基礎上創造 （漁）。這些圖像逐漸成為代替口語的符號和不經意地成為文字的雛形，然後經過許多年代的修改，才有系統的創造出大量的規範的文字。文字大概是這樣從無意識到有意識地創造出來的。

When the ancient Chinese used drawings to express ideas non-verbally, they were unknowingly beginning to create written characters. For example, the graphic represented the idea of a

魚 , “fish”, and the name of the object （yú, ㄩˊ）（please be noted there was no phonetic notation at that time yet）conveyed its pronunciation. Gradually, more and more graphics were created, such as adding elements to the original fish graphic （fish）to form （fishing） . These ancient graphics gradually evolved into the early forms of characters, initially created without the intention of our ancestors. Over many years of modification, these graphics were systematically developed into a large set of standardized characters. This is likely how Chinese characters evolved—from unconscious creation to deliberate design.

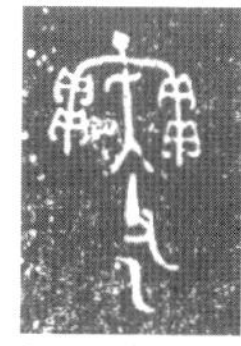

（摘自《漢字的文化史》，藤枝晃．日本）

古人表現生活形式的圖像。這些圖像都是未能確定是否會演變成文字。

Graphics showing the way of life of the ancient Chinese. It was uncertain whether these graphics would evolve into characters.

明顯地，古人畫圖像表現他們的生活形式和祭祀祖先，並無造字的意圖。部分圖像經過許多世代的反復修改才成為文字，這是意想不到的收穫。這個意外收穫催生了璀璨的中華文明。

Clearly, the ancients drew graphics to represent their way of life and to worship their ancestors, without any intention of creating characters. It is indeed unforeseen that some of these ancient graphics evolved into Chinese characters through the continuous revisions made by subsequent generations. This unexpected development contributed to the rise of the remarkable Chinese civilization.

四 漢字的特徵
Characteristics of Chinese Characters

15

由於漢字原來是可讀的圖畫，所以漢字具有形體、聲音、意義三個特徵。

Since Chinese characters originally began as readable graphics, they exhibit three characteristics: physical form, sound and meaning.

16

心 (**xīn**, ㄒㄧㄣ)

Heart

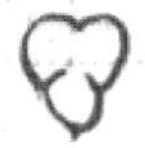 甲骨文	 金文	 篆書	 隸書	 楷書
Oracle bone script	Bronze script	Seal script	Clerical script	Regular Writing

三個特徵：

1. 形體：心的形狀。
2. 聲音：讀物名。
3. 意義：如圖像「心」。

Three characterics:

1. Physical form: the shape of the heart.
2. Sound: the name when pronounced (xīn, ㄒㄧㄣ).
3. Meaning: as represented by the graphic of "heart".

龜 **(gūi，ㄍㄨㄟ)**

Turtle

甲骨文	金文	篆書	隸書	楷書	簡體字
Oracle bone script	Bronze script	Seal script	Clerical script	Regular script	Simple form

三個特徵：

1. 形體：龜的形狀。
2. 聲音：讀物名。
3. 意義：如圖像「龜」。

Three characteristics:

1. Physical form: the shape of a turtle.
2. Sound : the name when pronounced（guī, ㄍㄨㄟ）.
3. Meaning: as represented by the graphic of “turtle”.

18

英文與漢字不同，它不具備象形的特徵，它只具有聲音和意義兩個特徵。

English is different from Chinese characters in that it does not possess pictographic features; it only has two characteristics: sound and meaning.

牛 (**niú, ㄋㄧㄡˊ**)

Cow

𐀀				
甲骨文	金文	篆書	隸書	楷書
Oracle bone script	Bronze script	Seal script	Clerical script	Regular script

漢字是通過圖像 → 牛 來表達字義，英文是通過發音 cow 來表達字義。它們的表達方式明顯的不同。

The meaning of a Chinese character is conveyed through its physical form, such as the character for "cow", → 牛 ; while in English, the meaning is expressed through its pronunciation, as in "cow". The difference in their modes of expression is quite evident.

五 從漢字結構看中華民族的倫常綱紀

Examining the Moral and Ethical principles of the Chinese Nation through the Structure of Chinese Characters

19

甲骨文的男性符號

Male symbol in oracle bone script

國際男性符號

International male symbol

祖 (**zǔ**, ㄗㄨˇ)

Ancestor

甲骨文	金文	篆書	隸書	楷書
Oracle bone script	Bronze script	Seal script	Clerical script	Regular script

中華民族的傳統宗教是祖靈信仰，拜祭祖宗。

The traditional religion of the Chinese nation is ancestor worship, which involves honoring and worshiping one's ancestors.

祖 字記錄了古人頂禮膜拜男性生殖器的儀式。

祖：二 是指「天與地」。

祖：小 代表「日、月、星」。

祖：示 指「天垂象」，即神的旨意。古人祭天地，所以「示」含有祭拜的意思。

祖：且 是男性生殖器象形。

《說文解字》說 祖 是「始廟」。

The character 祖（zǔ, ㄗㄨˇ）, "ancestor", records the ancient ritual of worshiping the male genitalia.

祖：二 represents "heaven and earth".

祖：小 represents "sun, moon and stars".

祖：示 theref ore collectively signifies "the heavenly bodies" that reflect divine guidance. In this context, it denotes "worship".

祖，且 is a pictograph of male genitalia.

According to *Shuowen Jiezi*, 祖 means "the ancestral temple".

20

孝（**xiào, ㄒㄧㄠˋ**）

filial piety

甲骨文	金文	篆書	隸書	楷書
Oracle bone script	Bronze script	Seal script	Clerical script	Regular script

百善孝為先，子女孝順長輩是中華民族的美德。

In Chinese tradition, filial piety is regarded as the highest virtue.

孝 字是由 老 字和 子 字合寫，「老」的地位高於「子」的地位，表示世代相傳和子女敬愛老一輩。

The character 孝（xiào, ㄒㄧㄠˋ）, “filial piety”, is a combination of the characters 老（lǎo, ㄌㄠˇ）, “elder”, and 子（zǐ, ㄗˇ）, “son”. The character 老（elder）is positioned above 子（son）, suggesting that life is passed down from generation to generation, and that the young should respect and love their elders.

21

君（君主）

(jūn, ㄐㄩㄣ)

monarch

甲骨文	金文	篆書	隸書	楷書
Oracle bone script	Bronze script	Seal script	Clerical script	Regular script

君權神授，所以君權至高無上。

「君」字甲骨文 = 手持權杖 + 口發號施令。

The divine right of kings is the doctrine that kings derive their authority from God. The character 君（jūn, ㄐㄩㄣ）, "monarch"（君主 jūn zhǔ, ㄐㄩㄣ ㄓㄨˇ）, in oracle bone script is . It represents a scepter held in hand and a verbal order , indicating the monarch's power is absolute.

22

臣（chén, ㄔㄣˊ）

official（under a feudal ruler）

甲骨文	金文	篆書	隸書	楷書
Oracle bone script	Bronze script	Seal script	Clerical script	Regular script

俯首稱臣，目不斜視，表示專注與聽從。所以「臣」字的甲骨文 表現「目不斜視」。

An official bows to his monarch without looking sideways, maintaining full focus on the monarch's words and demonstrating absolute deference. Thus, the character 臣（chén, ㄔㄣˊ）, "official"（under a feudal ruler）, in oracle bone script is . It represents "an eye looking neither to the right nor to the left".

23

男（**nán, ㄋㄢˊ**）

man

甲骨文	金文	篆書	隸書	楷書
Oracle bone script	Bronze script	Seal script	Clerical script	Regular script

在農業社會，男耕女織。男 = 田 + 力 → 犁田者為男人。

In agricultural societies, men plough the fields while women weave. The character 男（nán, ㄋㄢˊ）, "man", is formed by combining 田 , "field",and 力 , "plough". The one who ploughs the fields is a 男 , "man". You may see the character 男 on a lavatory door.

24

(nǔ, ㄋㄩˇ)

girl, lady, woman

			女	女
甲骨文	金文	篆書	隸書	楷書
Oracle bone script	Bronze script	Seal script	Clerical script	Regular script

「女」字的甲骨文 ，是一位行叉手禮，跪坐著，態度謙卑的女子。古人無椅子，他們席地而坐。

The character 女（nǔ, ㄋㄩˇ）, “girl”, “lady”, or “woman”, in oracle bone script is , which depicts a humble lady sitting in a kneeling position with her hands folded. Ancient people had no chairs; they sat on the ground.You may see the character 女 on a lavatory door.

25

母 (mǔ, ㄇㄨˇ)

mother

甲骨文	金文	篆書	隸書	楷書
Oracle bone script	Bronze script	Seal script	Clerical script	Regular script

在「女」字中加上兩點，便成為「母」字。這兩點是母親的乳房，因為母親需要餵奶。「有奶便是娘」原意是指餵奶的女人，當然是一位母親，正是這個「母」字的意思。這個成語形象地表現養育之恩，反而被用作貶義的成語，比喻貪利忘義，誰給好處就認誰為母。

By adding two dots to the oracle bone script for 女（nǚ，ㄋㄩˇ）, "woman", a new script for 母（mǔ，ㄇㄨˇ）, "mother", is invented. These two dots symbolize a mother's breasts, as she nurses her baby.

有奶便是娘（yǒu nǎi biān shì niáng，ㄧㄡˇㄋㄞˇ ㄅㄧㄢˋ ㄕˋ ㄋㄧㄤˊ）, literally means "a woman who nurses is by definition a mother". However, its figurative interpretation is "whoever feeds me is my mother”. This idiom is used to satirize people who bow to those who provide them with material benefits, regardless of moral principles.

對他來說，有奶便是娘

(duì tā lái shuō, yǒu nǎi biàn shì niáng，ㄉㄨㄟˋ ㄊㄚ ㄌㄞˊ ㄕㄨㄛ, ㄧㄡˇ ㄋㄞˇ ㄅㄧㄢˋ ㄕˋ ㄋㄧㄤˊ)

He obeys anyone who provides him with material benefits, regardless of moral principles.

26

毋 (wú, ㄨˊ)

never, absolutely not

甲骨文	金文	篆書	隸書	楷書
Oracle bone script	Bronze script	Seal script	Clerical script	Regular script

「毋」是「決不」的意思。「毋」字將「母」字的兩點乳房和下部私處劃一條線鎖住，表示「毋（決不允許）讓『母』被非禮或姦污」。

毋 means “never”or “not allowed”. The character 毋（wú，ㄨˊ）draws a line across 母（mǔ, ㄇㄨˇ）, “mother”, representing a strap blocking her breasts and private parts. It means “do not allow ‘mother’ to be violated or defiled”.

毋論斷人（wú lùn duàn rén, ㄨˋ ㄌㄨㄣˋ ㄉㄨㄢˋ ㄖㄣˊ）。

不可論斷人，不然，你會被論斷。（馬太福音 7:1 ，《聖經》）。

Judge not, that ye be not judged.（Matthew 7:1, King James Bible）.

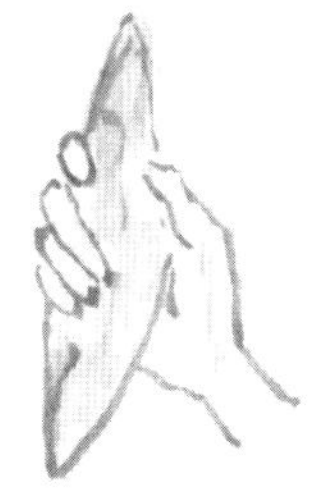

父（**fù,** ㄈㄨˋ）

Father

𠂇	𠂇	𠂇	父	父
甲骨文	金文	篆書	隸書	楷書
Oracle bone script	Bronze script	Seal script	Clerical script	Regular script

「父」字甲骨文 是石器時代手持石器工作的人。

父 （fù, ㄈㄨˋ），“father”, in oracle bone script is , representing a Stone Age man working with a stone tool in his hand .

28

夫 (**fū, ㄈㄨ**)

adult man, husband

夫	夫	夫	夫	夫
甲骨文	金文	篆書	隸書	楷書
Oracle bone script	Bronze script	Seal script	Clerical script	Regular script

「夫」、「丈夫」，甲骨文 ⼤ = 一個正面站立的漢子 ⼤ + 一 在頭髮部分插上一支標誌著成年的發簪。

夫（fū, ㄈㄨ），“adult man” or “husband”, in oracle bone script is ⼤ , representing a man standing upright and facing forward ⼤ , with a hairpin 一 （an important symbol of adulthood in ancient times） in his hair.

29

妻（qī, ㄑㄧ）

Wife

𡜏	𡜏	𡜏	妻	妻
甲骨文	金文	篆書	隸書	楷書
Oracle bone script	Bronze script	Seal script	Clerical script	Regular script

「妻」，甲骨文 = 一個女子， 她的頭髮被一隻手拽住，表示搶走這個女人來當作妻子。搶婚是古代的一種婚俗。

妻（qī, ㄑㄧ），“wife”, in oracle bone script is ，representing a lady with her hair being grasped by a hand . It signifies the act of seizing this woman to take her as a wife. Bride kidnapping was a customary practice in ancient times.

還有一個「娶」字，也是表現搶婦為妻。「娶」的甲骨文 是一隻手拽著一個女子的耳朵，搶走她來當作妻子。

There is another character 娶（qǔ ㄑㄩˇ），“marrying a woman”, which is also an expression of bride kidnapping. The oracle bone script for 娶 depicts a hand pulling a woman’s ear, symbolizing the act of taking her as a wife.

兄 (**xiōng,** ㄒㄩㄥ)

elder brother

甲骨文	金文	篆書	隸書	楷書
Oracle bone script	Bronze script	Seal script	Clerical script	Regular script

古時，兄長在家中有特權，可以指使弟弟和姐妹幹這個幹那個。所以「兄」字的甲骨文 是一個張開大口 發號施令的人。

In ancient times, the eldest brother held special privileges within the family and could command his younger siblings. Thus, the oracle bone script for “elder brother” is represented by a big mouth , signifying the act of speaking out commands.

31

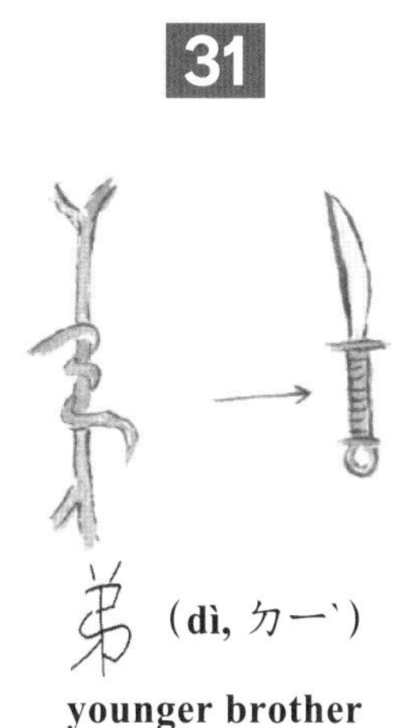

弟 (dì, ㄉㄧˋ)

younger brother

𢎨	𢎨	𢎨	弟	弟
甲骨文	金文	篆書	隸書	楷書
Oracle bone script	Bronze script	Seal script	Clerical script	Regular script

「弟」字的甲骨文 𢎨，是用一根繩索 己 一圈跟著一圈地纏繞在一支武器的手把上 𠂆，比喻兄弟關係不但緊密，而且排行有序，就好像這些繩圈一樣，一圈跟著一圈。「弟」的排行是這一圈跟著前一圈。

The oracle bone script 𢎨 for 弟（dì, ㄉㄧˋ）, "younger brother", depicts a rope 己 coiled around the handle of a weapon 𠂆 in overlapping circles. This imagery metaphorically illustrates that brotherly relationships are not only close but also ordered in hierarchy, much like the concentric loops of the rope. The order of 弟 signifies that each loop follows the previous one.

32

姐 (jiě, ㄐㄧㄝˇ)

elder sister

(無) (none)	(無) (none)	㛐	姐	姐
甲骨文	金文	篆書	隸書	楷書
Oracle bone script	Bronze script	Seal script	Clerical script	Regular script

「姐」字與「祖」字有點相似。在古代，「姐」是對外祖母的尊稱。後來，稱成婚的女子為「姐」。今「姐」為「姊」。

The character 姐（jiě, ㄐㄧㄝˇ）, "elder sister", is quite similar to the character 祖（zǔ, ㄗㄨˇ）, "ancestor". Indeed, in ancient times, 姐 was an honorific term for a maternal grandmother. Over time, 姐 evolved into the form of address for a married sister. Today, 姐 simply means "elder sister".

33

妹（mèi, ㄇㄟˋ）

younger sister

甲骨文	金文	篆書	隸書	楷書
Oracle bone script	Bronze script	Seal script	Clerical script	Regular script

「妹」字甲骨文 = 未結果的幼樹（象徵未成熟）+ 頭頂上結著一個標誌未婚女子的髮髻，表示留待家中未成年的女子。

妹（mèi, ㄇㄟˋ），“younger sister”, in oracle bone script is , depicting a young tree not yet bearing fruit（symbolizing imaturity）, and a girl in a hair bun signifying an unmarried maiden . It represents a girl who is not yet of age and is still living with her parents.

34

子 (**zǐ, ㄗˇ**)

child, son

𢀓	𢀓	𢀓	子	子
甲骨文	金文	篆書	隸書	楷書
Oracle bone script	Bronze script	Seal script	Clerical script	Regular script

「子」字的甲骨文 𢀓，是襁褓中的嬰孩，得到呵護。

The oracle bone script 𢀓 for 子（zǐ ㄗˇ）, "baby", is an infant in swaddling-clothes, who is being taken good care of.

35

好（hǎo, ㄏㄠˇ）/（hào, ㄏㄠˋ）

（adjective）good, nice, pretty /（verb）love, like

[illegible]	[illegible]	[illegible]	好	好
甲骨文	金文	篆書	隸書	楷書
Oracle bone script	Bronze script	Seal script	Clerical script	Regular script

好＝女＋子，因此有人認為好是男歡女愛。

好 “nice” or “love” = 女 “girl” or “lady” + 子 “boy” or “man”

Some assert that 好（hǎo, ㄏㄠˇ）consists of a woman 女 and a man 子 , essentially meaning “love”, as “goodness” arises when a woman and a man love each other passionately.

有人認為，一個家有女孩和男孩才是好。

Somebody believe that since 好（hǎo, ㄏㄠˇ）consists of a girl 女 and a boy 子, “goodness” stems from the idea of having both a daughter 女 and a son 子. Indeed, when Chinese parents have a daughter followed by a son, or vice versa, it is said that “goodness” is bestowed upon that family.

但是，真實含義應該是，好（形容詞）是指 女 子 漂亮好看，所以男子喜 好（動詞）。如在最古老的《詩經》裡所述的「窈窕淑女，君子好逑」。

However, the true meaning should be that 好（hǎo, ㄏㄠˇ）as an adjective refers to a 女 子（nǚ zǐ, ㄋㄩˇ ㄗˇ）, “lady”, who is beautiful, which is why men like her, 好（hào, ㄏㄠˋ）as a verb. This is echoed in the ancient（《詩經》shī jīng, ㄕ ㄐㄧㄥ）,“Book of Songs” , where it says “ 窈窕淑女（yǎo tiǎo shū nǚ, ㄧㄠˇ ㄊㄧㄠˇ ㄕㄨ, ㄋㄩˇ），君子好逑（jūn zǐ hào qiú ㄐㄩㄣ ㄗˇ ㄏㄠˋ ㄑㄧㄡˊ）”, meaning “a graceful and virtuous lady is the ideal match for a gentleman”.

Please note that the tones are different in pronunciation for 好（hǎo, ㄏㄠˇ）which is an adjective meaning ‘good, “nice”, or “pretty”,’and 好（hào, ㄏㄠˋ）, which is a verb meaning “to love”or “to like”.

同字不同義的詞語：

The same characters can convey different meanings depending on their arrangement in words:

女子（nǔ zǐ, ㄋㄩˇㄗˇ）: girl, lady, maiden

子女（zǐ nǔ, ㄗˇㄋㄩˇ）: kid, children

用「好」(hào, ㄏㄠˋ)（動詞）、「好」(hǎo, ㄏㄠˇ)（形容詞）及「女子」(nǔ zǐ, ㄋㄩˇㄗˇ）造一個句子：她好學，她是一個好女子。

Let's create a sentence that includes the verb 好（hào, ㄏㄠˋ）meaning "to love", the adjective 好（hǎo, ㄏㄠˇ）meaning "good", and the noun 女子（nǔ zǐ, ㄋㄩˇㄗˇ）meaning "girl".

她好（loves）學，她是一個好（good）女子（girl）。

（Tā hào xué, tā shì yī gè hǎo nǔ zǐ.

ㄊㄚ ㄏㄠˋ ㄒㄩㄝˊ, ㄊㄚ ㄕˋ ㄧ ㄍㄜˋ ㄏㄠˇ ㄋㄩˇㄗˇ。）

She loves to study, so she is a good girl.

36

家（jiā, ㄐㄧㄚ）

home, family

甲骨文	金文	篆書	隸書	楷書
Oracle bone script	Bronze script	Seal script	Clerical script	Regular script

「家」字甲骨文 = 「屋」+ 「豬」。古代，人們飼養馬、牛、羊、豬、狗、雞等六畜，只有豬是在「家」中圈養，所以 「屋」內有 「豬」便成了「家」的標誌。

家（jiā, ㄐㄧㄚ）, “home” or “family”, in oracle bone script is , consisting of a “house” and a “pig”. In ancient times, while horses, oxen, sheep, dogs, and chickens were already domesticated, only pigs were kept in pens inside the house. Thus, the character 家 is composed of “house” and “pig”. As a result, 家 has become a symbol of “home” and “family”.

Words:

回家（huí jiā, ㄏㄨㄟˊ ㄐㄧㄚ）: go home

我的家（wǒ de jiā, ㄨㄛˇ ㄉㄜ ㄐㄧㄚ）: my family

37

人 (rén, ㄖㄣˊ)

man, person

			人	人
甲骨文	金文	篆書	隸書	楷書
Oracle bone script	Bronze script	Seal script	Clerical script	Regular script

以禮待人是中國人的傳統美德。「人」字的甲骨文 ，是一個向別人作揖的人。

Treating others with courtesy is a traditional Chinese virtue. The oracle bone script for the character 人（rén, ㄖㄣˊ）, "person", depicts someone bowing with hands clasped in respect.

Words:

中國人（zhōng guó rén, ㄓㄨㄥ ㄍㄨㄛˊㄖㄣˊ）: Chinese

美國人（měi guó rén, ㄇㄟˇ ㄍㄨㄛˊㄖㄣˊ）: American

外國人（wài guó rén, ㄨㄞˋㄍㄨㄛˊㄖㄣˊ）: foreigner

六 一字多音

A Chinese Character can have Different Pronunciations in Various Dialects

38

漢字只有一種，但是漢語方言有數百種。雖然漢語方言同源，甚至許多漢語方言的聲母音或韻母音或聲調相近，但是這些方言之間不能互相交流。

While there is only one system of Chinese characters, there are hundreds of Chinese dialects, each capable of pronouncing the same characters in different ways. Although these dialects are related and may share similar consonants, vowels, or tones, oral communication between speakers of different dialects can often be extremely challenging.

你好 “hello” in

普通話 Putonghua: Ni Hao

粵語 Cantonese: Nei Hou

39

漢字是一字多音的，即是同一個漢字可以用不同的方言來讀，而它的意思不會因此改變，所以漢字成為維繫國家統一的紐帶。

A Chinese character can have multiple pronunciations across dialects, but its meaning remains unchanged. This consistency in meaning, despite pronunciation differences, allows Chinese characters to serve as a unifying bond across the nation.

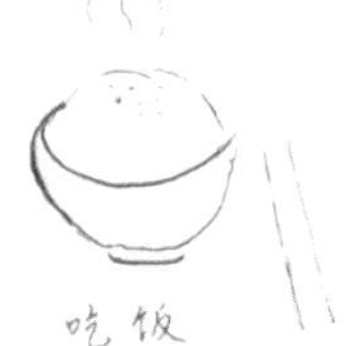

吃飯 **having a meal**

普通話 Putonghua: chī fàn

粵語 Cantonese: sik faan

閩南話 Hokkien: zia beng

上海話 Shanghainese: chiek van

40

普通話是全國通用口語。它以北京語音為標準音和以北方方言為基礎。全國推廣普通話。

Putonghua is the national spoken language in China. It is based on the Beijing pronunciation as the standard and draws from Northern dialects. Putonghua is promoted across the whole nation.

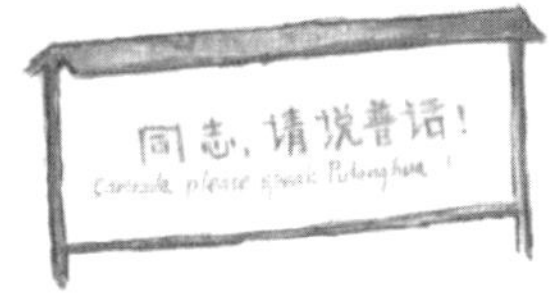

同志，請說普通話！

(tóngzhì, qǐng shuō pǔtōnghuà!

ㄊㄨㄥˊ ㄓˋ，ㄑㄧㄥˇ ㄕㄨㄛ ㄆㄨˇ ㄊㄨㄥ ㄏㄨㄚˋ！)

You might see the slogan「同志，請說普通話！」(“Comrades, please speak Putonghua！”) in some cities in Southern China.

41

普通話能不能最終代替其他方言？方言將來會走向滅絕嗎？這些是富有爭議性的課題。

幾千年的中國歷史，沒有因為方言分裂國家的事例。這是因為說同一種方言的人不一定都有相同的政治理念，所以方言本身沒有政治因素。秦始皇統一書體，但是沒有統一字音；康熙皇帝重視方言教學，他御定的《康熙字典》就提到「證鄉談法」，就是說如何用方言讀字；周恩來總理說：「推廣普通話，是為了消除方言之間的隔閡，而不是禁止和消滅方言」（周恩來：《當前文字改革的任務》，1958 年 1 月 10 日在政協全國委員會舉行的報告會上的報告），他還說：「方言是不能用行政命令來禁止，也不能用人為的辦法來消滅的……只會普通話的人，也要學點各地方言，才能深入各個方言區的勞動群眾。」

Will Putonghua eventually replace other dialects? Will dialects face extinction in the future? These are controversial topics.

Throughout thousands of years of Chinese history, there has been no evidence that dialects have caused national division. This is because speakers of the same dialect do not necessarily share the same political ideology; thus, dialects themselves do not carry political factors.

Emperor Qin Shi Huang unified the form of Chinese characters but did not standardize pronunciation. Emperor Kang Xi attached importance to Chinese dialects. The "Kang Xi Dictionary" describes how to read Chinese character in different dialects. Premier Zhou En Lai stated, "Promoting Putonghua is aimed at eliminating barriers between dialects, not at prohibiting or eradicating them"（Zhou Enlai: "The Current Tasks of Language Reform", Report at the National Committee of the Chinese People's Political Consultative Conference on January 10, 1958.）He also said, "Dialects cannot be banned by administrative orders, nor can they be eradicated by artificial means. Even those who only speak Putonghua should learn a bit of local dialects to engage with the working masses in different dialect areas. ”

42

大多數的南方人和東南亞的華人説粵語、客家話、閩南話、潮州話、海南話等等，這些都是漢語。在這些方言中，保留了不少古漢語的讀音。有時，用這些方言來吟古詩，比起普通話更為押韻。

Most Southerners and overseas Chinese in Southeast Asia speak the Chinese dialects of Cantonese, Hakka, Hokkien, Teochew, Hainanese, and so on. Many of these dialects preserve the authentic pronunciations of characters in the ancient Chinese language. As a result, reciting classical poetry in these dialects produces better rhymes compared to Putonghua.

春望（chūn wàngㄔㄨㄣ ㄨㄤˋ）
杜甫（西元 712-770）dù fǔㄉㄨˋㄈㄨˇ
國破山河在，
(guǒ pò shān hé zài，ㄍㄨㄛˇ ㄆㄛˋ ㄕㄢ ㄏㄜˊㄗㄞˋ,)
城春草木深。
(chéng chūn cǎo mù shēn。ㄔㄥˊㄔㄨㄣ ㄘㄠˋ ㄇㄨˋ ㄕㄣ。)
感時花濺淚，
(gǎn shí huā jiàn lèi，ㄍㄢˇ ㄕˊ ㄏㄨㄚ ㄐㄧㄢˋㄌㄟˋ,)

恨別鳥驚心。

（hèn bié niǎo jīng xīn。ㄏㄣˋㄅㄧㄝˊㄋㄧㄠˇㄐㄧㄥㄒㄧㄣ。）

烽火連三月，

（fēng huǒ lián sān yuè，ㄈㄥ ㄏㄨㄛˇㄌㄧㄢˊㄙㄢ ㄩㄝˋ。）

家書抵萬金。

（jiā shū dǐ wàn jīn。ㄐㄧㄚ ㄕㄨ ㄉㄧˇㄨㄢˋㄐㄧㄣ。）

白頭搔更短，

（bái tóu sāo gèng duǎn，ㄅㄞˊ ㄊㄡˊㄙㄠ ㄍㄥˋㄉㄨㄢˇ,）

渾欲不勝簪。

（huī yù bù shèng zān.ㄏㄨㄟ ㄩˋㄅㄨˋㄕㄥˋㄗㄢ。）

"Spring View" 春望 By Du Fu 杜甫（712-770 AD.）

The nation is broken, yet mountains and rivers remain,

In the City of Chang An in spring, grass and trees burgeon into lushness.

Touched by the times, even flowers are moved to tears,

As I lament the parting, my heart is frightened by the cries of birds.

The fire of war has lasted for three months,

A family letter is worth a million gold.

My greyed hair, becoming thinner as I scratch my head,

Is barely able to hold a hairpin up.

普通話讀起來，四個字不押韻，「深」（shēn, ㄕㄣ），「心」（xīn, ㄒㄧㄣ），「金」（jīn, ㄐㄧㄣ），「簪」（zān, ㄗㄢ）。

粵語就押韻，「深」sam，「心」sam，「金」gam，「簪」zam。

客家話也押韻，「深」qim，「心」sim，「金」gim，「簪」zim。

海南話也押韻，「深」xim，「心」dim，「金」gim，「簪」jium。

春望，"Spring View", is a famous poem by the renowned Tang Dynasty poet 杜甫 Du Fu. When recited in Putonghua, the ending characters of the even-numbered verses do not rhyme: 深（shēn, ㄕㄣ）, "lushness", 心（xīn, ㄒㄧㄣ）, "heart", 金（jīn, ㄐㄧㄣ）, "gold", 簪（zān, ㄗㄢ）, "hairpin".

In contrast, these characters do rhyme in Cantonese: 深（sam）, 心（sam）, 金（gam）, 簪（zam）.

They also rhyme in Hakka: 深（qim）, 心（sim）, 金（gim）, 簪（zim）.

Furthermore, in Hainanese, they rhyme as well: 深（xim）, 心（dim）, 金（gim）, 簪（jium）.

以上的例子在古代文章、詩詞中不勝枚舉。大多數的南方人和東南亞華人不懂得欣賞京劇和普通話相聲。

Similar examples abound in ancient literature and poetry. Most Southerners and overseas Chinese in Southeast Asia often struggle to appreciate Beijing operas and Putonghua talk shows.

43

為什麼用普通話來讀許多古詩詞，不押韻呢？原來有一些漢字的普通話讀音不是正宗的古漢語發音。西晉（西元 265 -316 年）末年，北方多個遊牧民族以及外族殺入中原，奪取西晉政權，形成了三百多年的「五胡亂華」政局，外族人學說的蹩腳的漢語成為北方方言，其發音特點是「南染吳越，北雜夷虜」（中古中原土著洛音沾染南邊江淮土著的吳音，而又夾雜著北邊胡人的語腔語調）其後，隨著各朝代國都的遷移，這種北方方言也隨之修正，北京是近代七、八百年的國都，所以北京方言成為今天流行的普通話。

Why do many ancient poems not rhyme when read in Putonghua? It turns out that some pronunciations in Putonghua do not align with the phonetic standards of the ancient Chinese language. The reasons are historical, tracing back to the end of the Western Jin Dynasty（265-316 AD）. Numerous nomadic tribes from China's northern borders, along with various ethnic minorities, began a 300-year-long invasion of the Central Plains to usurp the Western Jin throne, an era historically known as the "Turmoil of the Five Northern Minorities"（五胡亂華）. The broken Chinese spoken by these groups can be best described as a mix of the ancient Central dialect, the southern Jianghuai and Wu-Yue dialects, and the accents and intonations of the northern minorities. Over time, as China experienced relocations of its capital during the rise and fall of dynasties, these northern dialects underwent constant evolution, ultimately becoming the most widely spoken language in China today. The poorly spoken Chinese learned by these tribes became the Northern dialect.

Since Beijing has served as the capital for the last seven to eight hundred years, the Beijing dialect has become the foundation of the modern Putonghua we use today.

為什麼用南方方言唸古詩詞往往比較押韻呢？因為歷史上南方避過了「五胡亂華」，未受到胡人的語音影響，所以保留了南方古方言的聲韻與腔調。

This naturally raises the question: why do these ancient Chinese poems rhyme when recited in southern dialects? Historically, Southern China was spared the "Turmoil of the Five Northern Minorities"（五胡亂華）, and its dialects were unaffected by the accents and intonations of northern minorities. As a result, the ancient southern Chinese dialects have largely remained unchanged.

44

一字多音，多種方言共存是漢語應用的常態。
由於全國推廣普通話，外國朋友如要學習漢語口語就應該學習普通話。
為了便於與說各種不同方言的人溝通，就必須學好漢字。
In the Chinese language, it is very common for the same

character to be pronounced differently across dialects. Since Putonghua has been widely promoted nationwide, foreign learners are encouraged to learn it. To communicate effectively with speakers of different dialects in China, it is recommended to focus on learning Chinese characters.

45

漢語的一個最大特點是「書同文，語不同音」。漢字因此能夠在多方言的中國存活了幾千年。幾千年的經驗證明漢語做不到「既要書同文，又要語同音」。

A unique feature of the Chinese language is that each character has a single, unified written form, though it may have different pronunciations across dialects—something rarely seen in other languages. This consistency in written form has enabled Chinese characters to survive for thousands of years despite the diversity of dialects. Thousands of years of experience have shown that unifying the pronunciation of each character across dialects is practically impossible in China.

46

美國最早的華語播音是在 1939 年 2 月 18 日開始的粵語播音，後來才有國語播音，直至今日，每天均有粵語與國語播音。在世界二戰期間，美國曾有閩南語、潮州語播音。

The first Chinese radio broadcast in America was in Cantonese, beginning on February 18, 1939. Mandarin broadcasts followed later. Today, daily broadcasts are available in both Cantonese and Mandarin across the United States. Interestingly, during World War II, broadcasts in Hokkien and Teochew dialects were also aired in America.

七　一字多義

Chinese Character can have Multiple Meanings

47

說話時同音不同義的情況很多，所以漢語就有一字多義的現象。以「省」字為例：

A single Chinese character can have different meanings depending on the sentence or context. Many Chinese characters are homonyms, meaning they look and sound the same but carry different meanings. Take the character 省 (shěng, ㄕㄥˇ) as an example.

甲骨文	金文	篆書	隸書	楷書
Oracle bone script	Bronze script	Seal script	Clerical script	Regular script

「省」的原意是「視」。

The character 省（shěng, ㄕㄥˇ）originally means “to see” or “to view”.

一字多義

How the meanings of a single Chinese character vary depending on context:

省視（shěng shì, ㄕㄥˇ ㄕˋ）	To inspect
省親（shěng qīn, ㄕㄥˇ ㄑㄧㄣ）	To visit parents
省錢（shěng qián, ㄕㄥˇ ㄑㄧㄢˊ）	To save money
省略（shěng luè, ㄕㄥˇ ㄌㄩㄝˋ）	To omit
不省人事（bù shěng rén shì ㄅㄨˋ ㄕㄥˇ ㄖㄣˊ ㄕˋ）	unconscious
吾日三省吾身（wú rì sān sheng wú shēn。ㄨˊㄖˋ ㄙㄢ ㄕㄥˇ ㄨˊ ㄕㄣ）	“I examine myself three times a day.”
山東省（shān dōng sheng, ㄕㄢ ㄉㄨㄥㄕㄥˇ）	Shan Dong Province

一個漢字有多層意思，本書注解某字時，只能根據需要使用其中某個意思。

A single Chinese character can have multiple meanings; however, for the purposes of this book, only one meaning will be provided based on its context.

八 六書

Six Categories of Chinese Characters

48

古人經過數千年創造了大量的漢字。然後到了漢代（西元前 202 年 - 西元 220 年），學者們才將漢字的構成和使用方式歸類成六條例，即指事、象形、形聲、會意、轉注及假借等，稱之為「六書」。古人並不是先設定這六條例，然後照此造字。

Over thousands of years, the ancient Chinese created numerous characters. By the time of the Han Dynasty（202 BC – 220 AD）, scholars categorized these characters into six groups known as *Liushu* 六書（**liùshū, ㄌㄧㄡˋ ㄕㄨ**）**, or "Six Writing Forms". These categories are:（1）Self-explanatory characters,（2）Pictographic characters,（3）Pictophonetic characters,（4）Joint ideogram characters,（5）Mutually explanatory characters, and（6）Phonetic loan characters. However, many people mistakenly believe that these six categories were established prior to the creation of Chinese characters.**

(1) 指事
Self-explanatory characters

49

《說文解字》說，「指事者，視而可識，察而可見」。指事字是可以直接看懂，直接觀察到它的含義的。

Shuowen Jiezi **states, "Ideographic characters are recognizable at a glance and observable upon examination. " This indicates that ideographic characters can be directly understood and their meanings can be readily observed.**

大 **(dà,** ㄉㄚˋ**)**

Big

甲骨文	金文	篆書	隸書	楷書
Oracle bone script	Bronze script	Seal script	Clerical script	Regular script

「大」字的甲骨文是一個伸開雙臂雙腿站立的漢子，用身體語言表達「大」。人類是萬物之靈，是偉大的。

大（dà, ㄉㄚˋ）, "big", in oracle bone script, depicts a man standing with open arms and legs, a body language cue that conveys the concept of "big" or "great". This representation suggests that the Man embodies the essence of the universe, symbolizing both vastness and greatness.

天（**tiān, ㄊㄧㄢ**）

sky, heaven

甲骨文	金文	篆書	隸書	楷書
Oracle bone script	Bronze script	Seal script	Clerical script	Regular script

天字的甲骨文是指每個人頭頂上的空間。所有人都是頂天立地的。

天（tiān, ㄊㄧㄢ）, “sky” or “heaven”, is in oracle bone script. represents the space above everyone’s head, symbolizing that all individuals stand tall and firm between heaven and earth.

孕（yùn, ㄩㄣˋ）

pregnant

甲骨文	金文	篆書	隸書	楷書
Oracle bone script	Bronze script	Seal script	Clerical script	Regular script

孕字的甲骨文 是一個孕婦的透視圖。

孕（yùn, ㄩㄣˋ），“pregnant”, in oracle bone script, depicts a woman carrying a baby in her belly.

飞（**fēi,** ㄈㄟ）

Fly

甲骨文	金文	篆書	隸書	楷書	簡體字
Oracle bone script	Bronze script	Seal script	Clerical script	Regular script	Simple form

談到「飛」字，自然會想到鳥。「飛」字的甲骨文 是鳥兒展翅高飛。金文 是鳥兒沖天飛時，它的頸部和翅膀的羽毛充分張開。

When discussing the character 飛（fēi, ㄈㄟ）, "fly", we often envision a flying bird. Its oracle bone script shows a flying bird with widespread wings. In its Bronze script , the bird's neck and wing feathers are fully spread as it soars into the sky.

(2) 象形 Pictographic characters

53

《說文解字》說：「象形者，畫成其物，隨體詰詘」。象形字是簡化物象的複雜線條而描摹出來的大致模樣。

Shuowen Jiezi states, "Pictographs represent the form of the object, following its contours and nuances." A pictographic character is a simplified representation of complex lines that captures the general shape of an object.

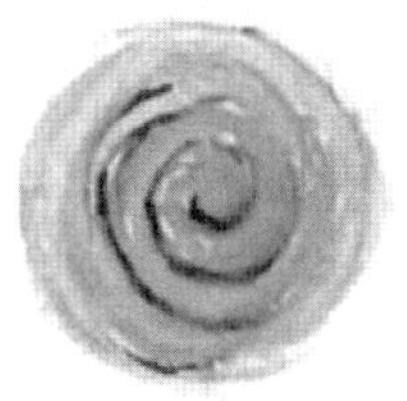

54

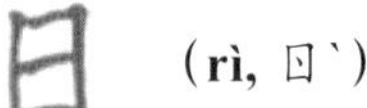

(rì, ㄖˋ)

sun, day

甲骨文	金文	篆書	隸書	楷書
Oracle bone script	Bronze script	Seal script	Clerical script	Regular script

日字的甲骨文是圓形的 ◎，其中的小圓圈是日影，日能投影。日出日落為一「日（天）」的時間。

日（rì, ㄖˋ），“sun”, is represented in oracle bone script as the round shape ◎. The small circle inside ◎ signifies the sun’s shadow, as the sun can cast shadows.

Additionally, 日 also means “day”, since the duration of a day is measured from sunrise to sunset.

55

月 **(yuè, ㄩㄝˋ)**

Moon, month

				月
甲骨文	金文	篆書	隸書	楷書
Oracle bone script	Bronze script	Seal script	Clerical script	Regular script

月圓時少，闕時多，所以甲骨文「月」字是圓缺。中一劃是月影，月也能投影。「月」繞地球一週為一個「月」的時間。

月（yuè, ㄩㄝˋ）, "moon", is crescent most of the time. Therefore its oracle bone script depicts a crescent moon, The stroke) inside signifies the moon's shadow, as the moon can cast shadows.

Additionally, 月 also means “month”, as it takes one month for the moon to complete a full revolution around the Earth.

56

陰陽圖

(yīn yáng tú, 一ㄣ一ㄤˊ ㄊㄨˊ)

Yin and Yang

古代哲學指自然界的一切事物都有正反對立的方面，一個代表反方面的是陰性，另一個代表正方面的是陽性。 -- 是陰爻的符號，它是雙符號； — 是陽爻的符號，它是單符號。

In ancient Chinese philosophy, Yin and Yang represent the two opposing principles in nature. Yin is associated with the negative or female element, while Yang is associated with the positive or male element. -- is the Yin symbol which is even. — is the Yang symbol which is odd.

月 字中的月影 = 如陰爻符號雙數 -- ，表示 月 是陰性。

The two strokes = that represents the moon’s shadow in 月（yuè, ㄩㄝˋ）, “moon”, are an even number similar to the Yin symbol ‐‐ . This indicates that the moon embodies the negative or female element.

日 字中的日影 — 如陽爻符號單數 — ，表示 日 是陽性。

The single stroke — that represents the sun's shadow in 日 (rì, ㄖˋ) , "sun", is an odd number similar to the Yang symbol — . This indicates that the sun embodies the positive or male element.

57

火 (**huǒ, ㄏㄨㄛˇ**)

Fire

𤆍	火	火	火	火
甲骨文	金文	篆書	隸書	楷書
Oracle bone script	Bronze script	Seal script	Clerical script	Regular script

甲骨文 → 火 的形狀，火焰向上抽。火 字中的兩點是

火星。

The oracle bone script for the character 火（huǒ, ㄏㄨㄛˇ）, “fire”, resembles flames rising upward. The two dots in 火 are sparks.

58

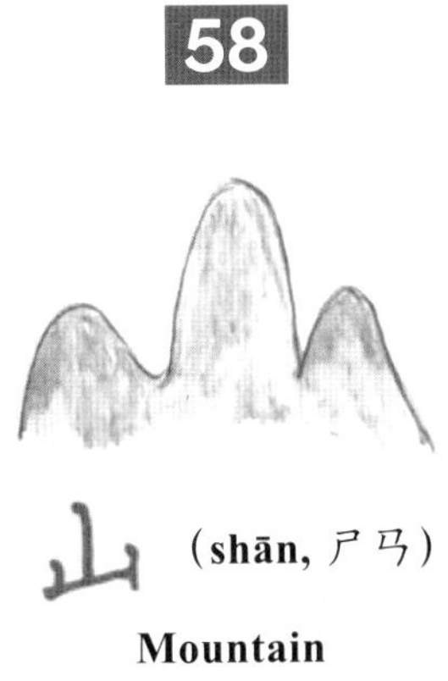

山（shān, ㄕㄢ）

Mountain

甲骨文	金文	篆書	隸書	楷書
Oracle bone script	Bronze script	Seal script	Clerical script	Regular script

山的甲骨文是三座山峰。「三」代表連綿的山巒。

The oracle bone script for the character 山（shān, ㄕㄢ）, “mountain”, depicts three mountain peaks. “Three”represents a series of continuous mountains.

(3) 形聲 Pictophonetic characters

59

《說文解字》說：「形聲者，以事為名，取譬相成」。形聲字是用關聯意義的字或部首，以及關聯語音的字互相組成。

Shuowen Jiezi states, “Pictophonetic characters are named after things, using meaning and sound to complement each other.” Pictophonetic characters are formed by combining characters or radicals that provide meanings, with characters that provide sounds. A pictophonetic character is thus composed of a meaning element and a sound element.

60

糕 (**gāo,** ㄍㄠ)

Cake

糕 → 米 表示字義。羔是讀音。

米 的甲骨文 ⺌（一根稻草、六粒稻米），「米」代表五穀雜糧。糕 是用五穀雜糧做成的。羔是注音，糕讀 羔 音，並無羔的意思。

The oracle bone script ⺌ for 糕（gāo, ㄍㄠ）, “cake”, resembles six grains of rice on a single straw. 米（mǐ, ㄇㄧˇ）, “rice”，is the meaning element, as 米 represents various grains, which is what 糕 is made of. On the other hand, 羔 is the sound element. Although 糕 is pronounced as 羔（gāo, ㄍㄠ）, it does not mean 羔 , “lamb”.

61

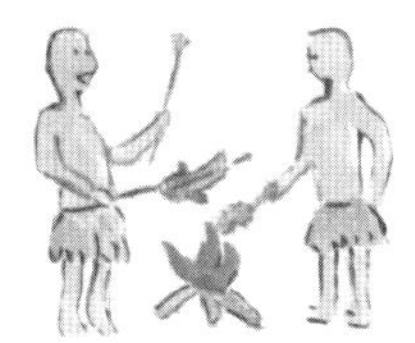

伙（huǒ, ㄏㄨㄛˇ）

fellow, partner

伙 → 亻（甲骨文 亻「人」）表示字義，指某種人。火是讀音。

伙讀火音，但是沒有火的意思。

一組人在一堆火邊燒烤，所以 伙是 亻「人」在火旁，表示這組人同吃一堆火燒烤的食物，他們是同火（伙）人。

Consider the character 伙（huǒ, ㄏㄨㄛˇ）, “fellow” or “partner”. Its meaning element is 亻, whose oracle bone script depicts a certain group of people.

On the other hand, its sound element is 火, whose oracle bone script depicts fire. Although 伙 is pronounced as 火（huǒ，ㄏㄨㄛˇ）, it does not mean 火, “fire”.

伙 is made of 亻 and 火, “people” beside “fire”. A group of people barbecuing around a fire are fellows 伙.

詞語 Words:

伙食（huǒ shí,ㄏㄨㄛˇ ㄕˊ）“communal meals”

Meals shared by a group of people, typically soldiers, students, factory workers, or others who regularly dine together.

伙 記（huǒjì, ㄏㄛˇㄐㄧˋ）“fellow”

Even today, Hong Kong policemen refer to their colleagues as 伙記（huǒjì, ㄏㄛˇㄐㄧˋ）, meaning “fellows”.

團伙（tuán huǒ, ㄉㄨㄢˊ ㄏㄨㄛˇ）“gangster”

合伙人（hé huǒ rén , ㄏㄜˊ ㄏㄨㄛˇ ㄖㄣˊ）“partner”

(4) 會意
Joint Ideogram Characters

62

《說文解字》說：「會意者，比類合誼，見類指撝」。會意字是適宜地會合數字的意義，從而見到所指的含義。

Shuowen Jiezi states, "Joint ideogram characters are created by combining two or more characters to form a new meaning." Joint ideogram characters effectively merge the meanings of their components, allowing one to figure out the intended meaning.

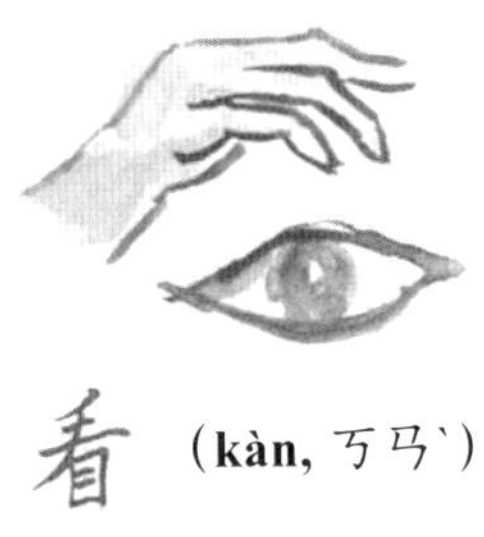

看 **(kàn,** ㄎㄢˋ**)**

look

(無) (none)	(無) (none)	[illegible]	看	看
甲骨文	金文	篆書	隸書	楷書
Oracle bone script	Bronze script	Seal script	Clerical script	Regular script

看 = 手 + 目 → 用手為目遮擋陽光，朝前看。

看（kàn, ㄎㄢˋ），"look" = 手 "hand" + 目 "eye". It means raising a hand to shade the eyes from sunlight while looking forward.

63

休（xiū, ㄒㄧㄡ）

taking a rest

甲骨文	金文	篆書	隸書	楷書
Oracle bone script	Bronze script	Seal script	Clerical script	Regular script

休字甲骨文 = 亻 + 木 → 一個人在樹蔭下休息。

Let's consider the character 休（xiū, ㄒㄧㄡ），"taking a rest".

Its oracle bone script = "man" + "tree".

It indicates a man taking a rest under a tree.

嬲 (niǎo, ㄋㄧㄠˇ)

嬲 字，當兩男夾著一女，將會發生什麼情況呢？表現兩個男人爭風吃醋。

Let's look at the character 嬲 （niǎo ㄋㄧㄠˇ）. When a lady 女 is sandwiched between two men 男 ，how will the men act？ represents two men's jealousy over a lady.

嬲 字的幾個意思：

The character 嬲（niǎo，ㄋㄧㄠˇ）has several meanings:

嬲：戲弄 tease

他們嬲一位靚女。

（tāmén niǎo yīwèi liàngnǚ 。

ㄊㄚ ㄇㄣˊ ㄋㄧㄠˊ ㄧ ㄨㄟˋ ㄌㄧㄤˋ ㄋㄩˇ 。）

They are teasing a beautiful lady.

嬲：騷擾 harass

他們嬲一位婦人。

(tāmén niǎo yīwèi fùrén。

ㄊㄚ ㄇㄣˊ ㄋㄧㄠˊ ㄧㄨㄟˋ ㄈㄨˋㄖㄣˊ。)

They are harassing a woman.

嬲：生氣 angry

他們為了一個女人而嬲。

(tāmén wèilē yīgè nǚrén ér niǎo。

ㄊㄚ ㄇㄣˊ ㄨㄟˋㄌㄜ ㄧㄍㄜˋ ㄋㄩˇㄖㄣˊ ㄦˊㄋㄧㄠˊ。)

They are angry with each other because of a lady.

65

嫐 (**nǎo**，ㄋㄠˇ)

嫐 字，當兩女之間有一男時，情況又如何？ 表現兩個女人爭風吃醋。

Let's look at the character 嬲 (nǎo, ㄋㄠˇ). When two ladies 女 are together with a man 男, how will the ladies act? 嬲 represents two ladies' jealousy over a man.

嬲：嬌媚 flirt
那些女人嬲他。
（Nèxiē nǚrén nǎo tā。
ㄋㄜˋㄒㄧㄝˊㄋㄩˇㄖㄣˊㄋㄠˇ ㄊㄚ。）
Those ladies are flirting with him.

(5) 轉注 Mutually Explanatory Characters

66

《說文解字》說：「轉注者，建類一首，同意相受。」轉注字是同一類部首，同樣意義的可以互訓（相同解釋和可以互相替代）的字。

Shouwen Jiezi states, "Mutually explanatory characters have the same radicals, sharing similar meanings." Mutually explanatory characters are synonyms that share the same radicals and can be substituted for one another in a sentence.

67

爹（diē, ㄉㄧㄝ）, father or Dad ⇌ 爸（bà, ㄅㄚˋ）, father or Papa 爹和爸是轉注字，同是 父 部首，同樣是父親的意思，是可以替換使用的。

爹（diē, ㄉㄧㄝ）, “father” or “Dad”, and 爸（bà, ㄅㄚˋ）“father” or “Papa”, are mutually explanatory characters. They are synonyms with the same radical 父 , “father”. They can be substituted for each other in a sentence.

提（tí, ㄊㄧˊ）hand-carry ⇌ 拎（líng,ㄌㄧㄥˊ）hand-carry

提和拎是轉注字，同樣是 扌（手）部首的同義字。是可以替換使用的。

提（yí, ㄊㄧˊ），“hand-carry”, and 拎（líng, ㄌㄧㄥˊ），“hand-carry”, are mutually explanatory characters. They are synonyms with the same radical 扌，“hand”. They can be substituted for each other in a sentence.

(6) 假借

Phonetic Loan Characters

69

《說文解字》說：「假借者，本無其字，依聲托事。」有時口裡能說出來的意思，但是無法造字來表達它，這時只好借用同音的字來表達。這些被借用的字是假借字。

Shuowen Jiezi states, “Phonetic loan characters are those that originally do not have a corresponding character, and are borrowed to express meaning based on similar sounds. ” Some concepts can be orally expressed but cannot be represented by existing characters; in such cases, a homophonous character is borrowed to convey the idea. These borrowed characters are known as phonetic loan characters.

When a character is "loaned" from another, it retains the same written form and pronunciation but has a different meaning.

花 (**huā,** ㄏㄨㄚ)

flower

			花	花	花
甲骨文	金文	篆書	隸書	楷書	簡體字
Oracle bone script	Bronze script	Seal script	Clerical script	Regular script	Simple Form

花是一個象形字。

人們口中所說的「花費」的「花」與「花草」的「花」的意思是不同的。真是沒有辦法造出一個字來表示「花費」的「花」。這時只好借用同音字「花草」的「花」字來表達「花費」的「花」的意思了。所以「花費」的「花」是一個假借字，它從「花草」那裡借來「花」字，它與「花草」的「花」字雖然同字形又同字音，但是意思不同。

花（huā, ㄏㄨㄚ）, “flower”, is a pictographic character.

When 花（huā, ㄏㄨㄚ）means “to spend”, it serves as a phonetic loan character. There is no specific character in Chinese to represent the oral expression of “to spend”. However, since the pronunciation for “to spend” is the same as that of 花（huā, ㄏㄨㄚ）, “flower”, the character 花 is phonetically “loaned” to convey the meaning of “to spend”.

他花錢買花送給她。

（tā huā qián mǎi huā sòng gěi tā。

ㄊㄚ ㄏㄨㄚ ㄑㄧㄢˇ ㄇㄞˇ ㄏㄨㄚ ㄙㄨㄥˋ ㄍㄟˇㄊㄚ。）

He <u>spends</u> 花（huā, ㄏㄨㄚ）money to buy <u>flowers</u> 花（huā, ㄏㄨㄚ）for her.

我花三年時間寫完這本書。

（wǒ huā sān nián shíjiān xiě wán zhè běn shū。

ㄨㄛˇ ㄏㄨㄚ ㄙㄢ ㄋㄧㄢˊ ㄕˊㄐㄧㄢ ㄒㄧㄝˇ ㄨㄢˊ ㄓㄜˋㄅㄣˇ ㄕㄨ。）

I <u>spent</u> 花（huā ㄏㄨㄚ）three years to write this book.

71

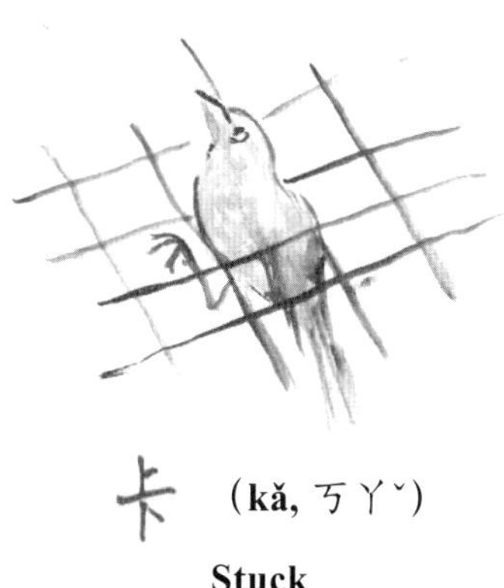

卡 (**kǎ, ㄎㄚˇ**)

Stuck

卡 是一個會意字，不上不下，卡住了。

卡（kǎ, ㄎㄚˇ）, "stuck", is a joint ideogram character. It is created by combining the characters 上 "up" and 下 "down". It vividly conveys the idea of being suspended in midair.

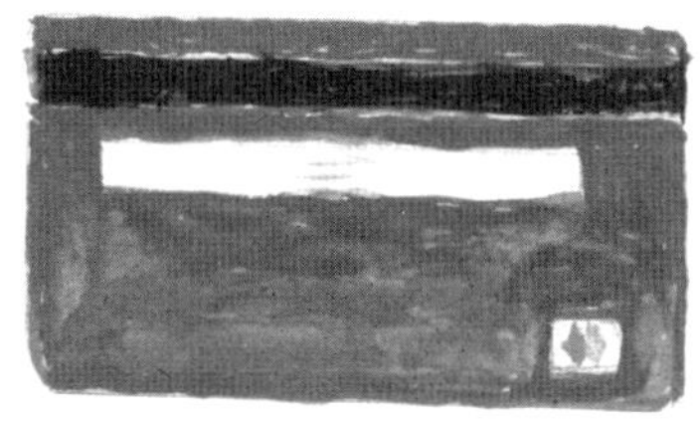

卡 (**kǎ, ㄎㄚˇ**)

card

信用卡

(**xìn yòng kǎ** ㄒㄧㄣˋ ㄩㄥˋ ㄎㄚˇ)

credit card

信用卡的卡字是假借字。

When 卡（kǎ, ㄎㄚˇ）means “card” as in 信用卡, “credit card”, it serves as a phonetic loan character.

九 國際交通標誌與漢字的比較

Comparison between International Traffic Signs and Chinese Characters

72

國際交通標誌是「超語言」的，即是說，可以用任何語言來讀它們。這是因為它們是指事的標誌、象形的標誌和會意的標誌，所以容易看懂。漢字裡的指事、象形和會意的單字雖然不如國際交通標誌那麼明顯的看得懂，但是，實質上它們和國際交通標誌一樣，也是「超語言」的，可以直接用任何語言來讀它們。

International traffic signs are language-free, meaning they can be understood regardless of the language spoken, as they are either self-explanatory, pictographic, or joint ideogram signs. Similarly, Chinese characters that are self-explanatory, pictographic, or joint ideograms can also be read across languages, although they may not be as immediately recognizable as international traffic signs.

正是因為漢字的這些特點，在古代部分漢字才能被越南、韓國、日本借用為自己的文字。例如，魚（ ）字都被這三個國家借用，均可用各自的語言來唸，越語「cá」、韓語「saengseon」、日語「sakana」。

In ancient times, some Chinese characters were loaned by Vietnam, Korea and Japan, precisely because they can be read across languages. For example, 魚（ ）, "fish", has been loaned by all three countries and can be pronounced in their respective languages: "cá" in Vietnamese, "saengseon" in Korean, and "sakana" in Japanese.

(1) 指事的單字與指事的交通標誌一樣，是可以直接用任何語言來讀的。
Like self-explanatory traffic signs, single Chinese self-explanatory characters can be read in any language.

73

用向左箭頭表示方向，是一個指事的標誌。任何人都能看得懂，並能用自己的語言來讀它。

The left arrow indicates direction and serves as a self-explanatory sign. Anyone can understand it and read it in their own language.

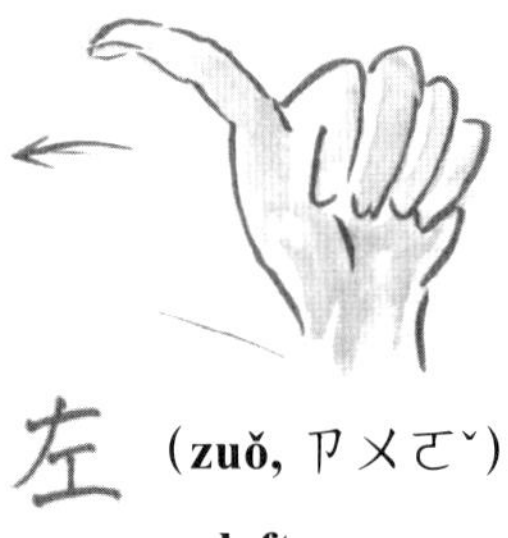

左 **(zuǒ, ㄗㄨㄛˇ)**

left

甲骨文	金文	篆書	隸書	楷書
Oracle bone script	Bronze script	Seal script	Clerical script	Regular script

漢字左字的甲骨文是畫左手來表示方向，是一個指事字，所以可以直接用任何語言來讀它，例如，左 可以直接讀 left（英語）、izquierda（西班牙語）、gauche（法語）、linke（德語）、sinistra（義大利語）等等。相反，left（英語）、izquierda（西班牙語）、gauche（法語）、linke（德語）、sinistra（義大利語）等就不能直接用其他語言來讀，只能按照其拼音來讀。

The character 左 , “left”, represented by a left hand showing direction in its oracle bone script , is a self-explanatory character that can be directly read and understood in any language.

For instance, 左 can be directly read as "left" in English, "izquierda" in Spanish, "gauche"in French, "linke" in German, "sinistra"in Italian, and so on. In contrast, the words "left", "izquierda", "gauche", "linke", and "sinistra" cannot be read in other languages without relying on their spelling.

用向右箭頭表示方向，是一個指事的標誌。任何人都能看得懂，並能用自己的語言來讀它。

The right arrow indicates direction and serves as a self-explanatory sign. Anyone can understand it and read it in their own language.

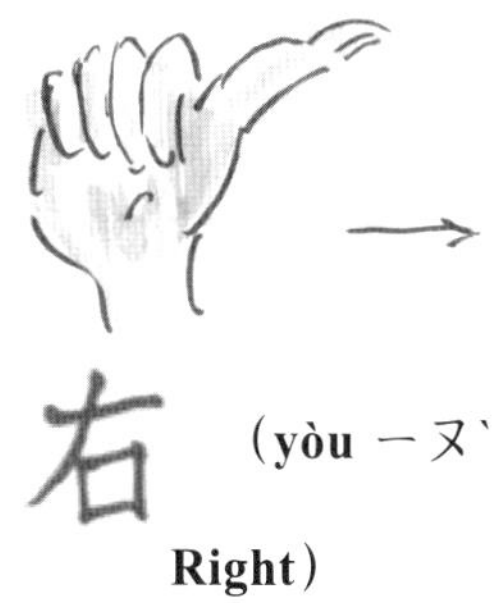

			右	右
甲骨文	金文	篆書	隸書	楷書
Oracle bone script	Bronze script	Seal script	Clerical script	Regular script

漢字 右 字甲骨文是畫右手 來表示方向，是一個指事字，可以直接用任何語言來讀它，例如，右 可以直接讀 right（英語）、derecha（西班牙語）、droit（法語）、recht（德語）、destra（義大利語）等等，相反，right（英語）、derecha（西班牙語）、droit（法語）、recht（德語）、destra（義大利語）等就不能直接用其他語言來讀，只能按照其拼音來讀。

The character 右 , “right”, represented by a right hand showing direction in its oracle bone script , is a self-explanatory character that can be directly read and understood in any language.

For instance, 右 can be directly read as “right” in English, “derecha”in Spanish, “droit” in French, “recht” in German, “destra” in Italian, and so on. In contrast, the words “right”, “derecha”, “droit”, “recht”, and “destra”cannot be read in other languages without relying on their spelling.

75

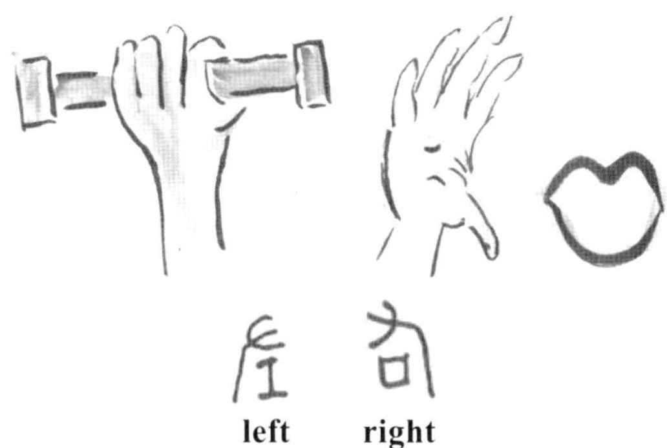

「左」與「右」字的關聯，獵人左手提著工具，右手圍著口呼喊。

The Bronze scripts and , for 左（"left"）, and 右（"right"）respectively, are closely related. A hunter is holding a tool in his left hand and shouting with his right hand partially cupped to his mouth.

76

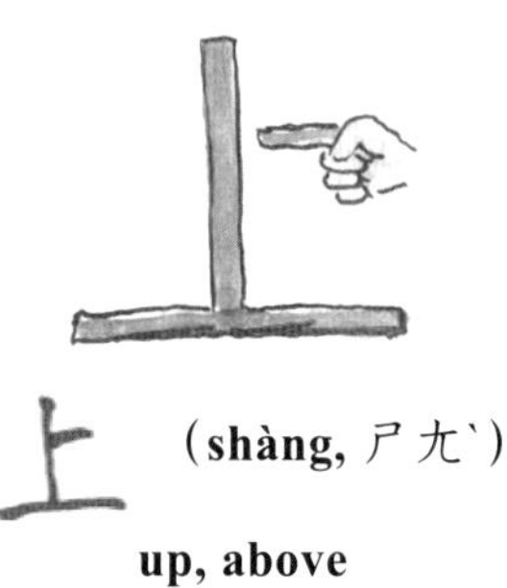

上 (shàng, ㄕㄤˋ)

up, above

甲骨文	金文	篆書	隸書	楷書
Oracle bone script	Bronze script	Seal script	Clerical script	Regular script

甲骨文「上」字，其上面的短線代表天，下面的長線代表地，原意是「上」者如天對地而言，所以「上」是一個指事字，是可以直接用任何語言來讀它的，例如，「上」可以直接讀 above（英語）、arriba（西班牙語）、haut（法語）、auf（德語）、sopra（義大利語）等等，相反，above（英語）、arriba（西班牙語）、haut（法語）、auf（德語）、sopra（義大利語）等就不能直接用其他語言來讀，只能按照其拼音來讀。

The character 上, “up” or “above”, in oracle bone script, depicts a short stroke above and a long stroke below. The upper short stroke represents the sky, while the lower long stroke represents the earth, signifying that the sky is above the earth. Thus, 上 is a self-explanatory character that can directly read and understood in any language.

For instance, 上 can be directly read as "above" in English, "arriba" in Spanish, "haut" in French, "auf" in German, "sopra" in Italian, and so on. In contrast, the words "above", "arriba", "haut", "auf" and "sopra"cannot be read in other languages without relying on their spelling.

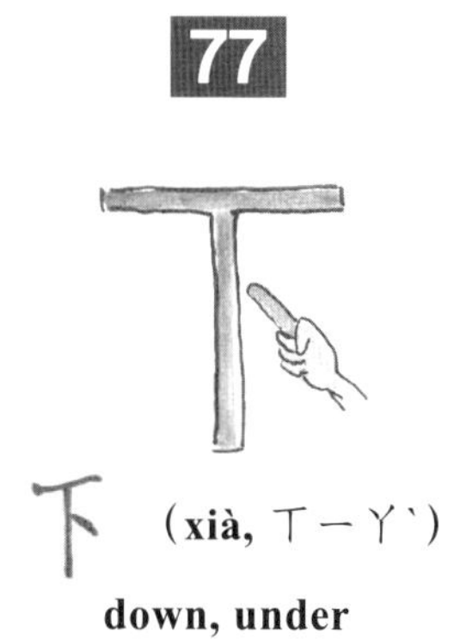

77

下 (**xià,** ㄒㄧㄚˋ)

down, under

甲骨文	金文	篆書	隸書	楷書
Oracle bone script	Bronze script	Seal script	Clerical script	Regular script

甲骨文 「下」，其下面的短線代表地，上面的長線代表天，原意是「下」者如地對天而言，所以「下」是一個指事

字，是可以直接用任何語言來讀的，例如，「下」可以直接讀 under（英語）、abajo（西班牙語）、bas（法語）、unter（德語）、sotto（義大利語）等等。相反，under（英語）、abajo（西班牙語）、bas（法語）、unter（德語）、sotto（義大利語）等就不能直接用其他語言來讀，只能按照其拼音來讀。

The character 下, “down” or “under”, in oracle bone script, depicts a short stroke below and a long stroke above. The lower short stroke represents the earth, while the upper long stroke represents the sky, signifying the earth is below the sky. Thus, 下 is a self-explanatory character that can directly read and understood in any language.

For instance, 下 can be directly read as “under” in English, “abajo” in Spanish, “bas” in French, “unter” in German, “sotto”in Italian, and so on. In contrast, the words “under”, “abajo”, “bas”, “unter” and “sotto” cannot be read in other languages without relying on their spelling.

(2) 象形單字與象形的交通標誌一樣，是可以直接用任何語言來讀的。
Like pictographic traffic signs, single Chinese pictographic characters can be read in any language.

78

不言而喻，任何人都能看懂的象形

This pictographic traffic sign is self-evident and can be understood by anyone.

你能看出這個甲骨文是鹿的象形嗎？

Can you see that is the oracle bone script for「deer」？

鹿 (lù，ㄌㄨˋ)

Deer

甲骨文	金文	篆書	隸書	楷書
Oracle bone script	Bronze script	Seal script	Clerical script	Regular script

「鹿」是象形字，和一樣，是可以直接用任何語言來讀它的，例如，「鹿」可以直接讀 deer（英語）、ciervo（西班牙語）、cerf（法語）、hirsch（德語）、cervo（義大利語）等等。相反，deer（英語）、ciervo（西班牙語）、cerf（法語）、hirsch（德

語）、cervo（義大利語）等就不能直接用其他語言的發音來讀，只能按照其拼音來讀。

鹿，“deer”, whose oracle bone script is , is a pictographic character.

Like the traffic sign , it can be directly read and understood in any language. For instance, 鹿 can be directly read as “deer” in English, “ciervo”in Spanish, “cerf” in French, “hirsch” in German, “cervo” in Italian, and so on. In contrast, the words “deer”, “ciervo”, “cerf”, “hirsch”and “cervo” cannot be read in other languages without relying on their spelling.

79

象 elephant

不言而喻，任何人都能看懂的象形。

This pictographic traffic sign is self-evident and can be understood by anyone.

你能看出這個甲骨文 是 的象形嗎？

Can you see that is the oracle bone script for “ elephant ”?

(xiàng，ㄒㄧㄤˋ)

elephant

甲骨文	金文	篆書	隸書	楷書
Oracle bone script	Bronze script	Seal script	Clerical script	Regular script

「象」是象形字，和 一樣，是可以用任何語言來讀它的，例如，「象」可以直接讀 elephant（英語）、elefante（西班牙語）、éléphant（法語）、elefant（德語）、elefante（義大利語）等等。相反，elephant（英語）、elefante（西班牙語）、éléphant（法語）、elefant（德語）、elefante（義大利語）等就不能直接用其他語言來讀，只能按照其拼音來讀。

象, “elephant”, with the oracle bone script , is a pictographic character.

Like the traffic sign , it can be directly read and understood in any language. For instance, 象 can be directly read as "elephant" in English, "elefante" in Spanish, "éléphant"in French, "elefant" in German, "elefante" in Italian, and so on. In contrast, the words "elephant", "elefante", "éléphant", "elefant" and "elefante" cannot be read in other languages without relying on their spelling.

80

十二生肖字都是象形字，是可以用任何語言來讀的。下面漢字，你可以用任何語言來讀。請將不同的語言文字寫在括弧內。

The characters for the twelve Chinese zodiac animals are pictographic and can be directly read in any language. You can try to read them using your native language or any other language you are familiar with. Please fill in the blanks with the corresponding words（if not English）:

	鼠	rat	[ ]		牛	ox	[ ]
	虎	tiger	[ ]		兔	rabbit	[ ]
	龍	dragon	[ ]		蛇	snake	[ ]
	馬	horse	[ ]		羊	goat	[ ]
	猴	monkey	[ ]		雞	rooster	[ ]
	犬	dog	[ ]		豕	pig	[ ]

(3) 會意單字與會意的交通標誌一樣，是可以用任何語言來讀的

Like joint ideogram traffic signs, single Chinese joint ideogram characters can be read in any language.

81

小心！保護小孩。

這個交通標誌用「大人 + 小孩 」會意「保護」。

Warning! Adult and child crossing. Please protect the children. An adult is holding the hand of a child . This sign instructs drivers to "protect"children by driving more cautiously.

保 **(bǎo, ㄅㄠˇ)**

protect

			保	保
甲骨文	金文	篆書	隸書	楷書
Oracle bone script	Bronze script	Seal script	Clerical script	Regular script

你覺得這個金文 與 相似嗎？它就是保字。

Doesn't the Bronze script for 保 look like ? It means "to protect".

「保」是會意字，和交通標誌 一樣，是可以用任何語言來讀的。例如，「保」可以直接讀 protect（英語）、proteger（西班牙語）、protéger（法語）、schutz（德語）、protezione（義大利語）等等。相反，protect（英語）、proteger（西班牙語）、protéger（法語）、schutz（德語）、protezione（義大利語）等就不能直接用其他語言來讀，只能按照其拼音來讀。

保, "protect", whose Bronze script is , is a joint ideogram character.

Like the traffic sign , it can be directly read and understood in any language. For instance, 保 can be directly read as "protect" in English, "proteger" in Spanish, "protéger" in French, "schutz" in German, "protezione" in Italian, and so on. In contrast, "protect", "proteger", "protéger", "schutz" and "protezione" cannot be read in other languages without relying on their spelling.

82

灾（zāi，ㄗㄞ）

Disaster

			灾	灾
甲骨文	金文	篆書	隸書	楷書
Oracle bone script	Bronze script	Seal script	Clerical script	Regular script

甲骨文（災）→屋內著火→會意「災」

The oracle bone script for 災, “disaster”, depicts a “house” on “fire”.

「災」是會意字，是可以用任何語言來讀它的。例如，「災」可以直接讀 disaster（英語）、desastre（西班牙語）、catastrophe（法語）、katastrophe（德語），disasto（義大利語）等等任何語言。相反，disaster（英語）、desastre（西班牙語）、catastrophe（法語）、katastrophe（德語）、disasto（義大利語）就不能直接用其他語言來讀，只能按照其拼音來讀。

災, “disaster”, whose oracle bone script is , is a joint ideogram character. It can be directly read and understood in any language. For instance, 災 can be directly read as "disaster" in English, "desastre" in Spanish, "catastrophe"in French, "katastrophe" in German, "disasto" in Italian, and so on. In contrast, "disaster", "desastre", "catastrophe", "katastrophe" and "disasto" cannot be read in other languages without relying on their spelling.

(4)由兩個或以上個字組成的詞語只能讀漢語音 Words composed of two or more characters can only be read in Chinese pronunciation

83

由兩個或以上個字組成的詞語，只能用漢語來讀。

例如：火車（huǒ chē，ㄏㄨㄛˇ ㄔㄜ）

英語不能讀成 fire car

電腦（diàn nǎo，ㄉㄧㄢˋ ㄋㄠˇ）

英語不能讀成 electrical brain

電動車（diàn dòng chē，ㄉㄧㄢˋ ㄉㄨㄥˋ ㄔㄜ）

英語不能讀成 electrical motor car

It is important to note that words composed of two or more characters can only be expressed orally in Chinese.

For example,

火車（huǒ chē，ㄏㄨㄛˇ ㄔㄜ）train.

You cannot read 火車 directly from its characters as "fire car".

電腦（diàn nǎo，ㄉㄧㄢˋ ㄋㄠˇ）computer.

You cannot read 電腦 directly from its characters as "electrical brain".

電動車（diàn dòng chē，ㄉㄧㄢˋ ㄉㄨㄥˋ ㄔㄜ）motorcycle.

You cannot read 電動車 directly from its characters as"electrical motor car".

(5)並非所有的漢字都是「超語言」的 Not all Chinese Characters are Language-Free

84

形聲字和假借字只能讀漢語音，而不能用其他語言來讀。

Pictophonetic characters and phonetic loan characters can only be read in Chinese, not in other languages.

因為形聲字的聲是漢語的音聲，所以只能用漢語來讀，不能直接用外語來讀。

Since the sound element of pictophonetic characters is specific to Chinese phonetics, they can only be read in Chinese.

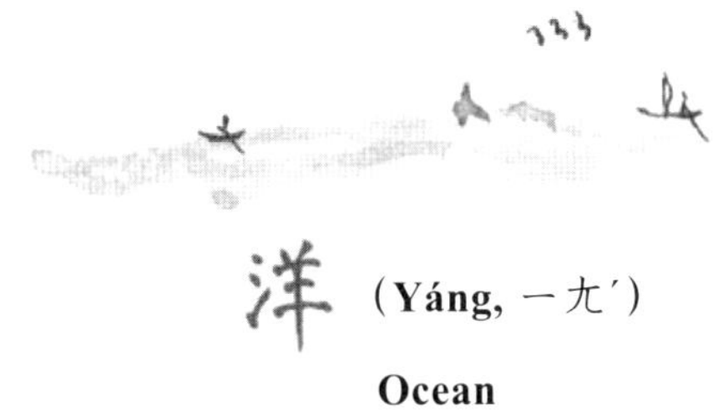

洋 (**Yáng, 一ㄤˊ**)

Ocean

洋 是一個形聲字，氵代表水，羊（yang, 一ㄤ）是漢語的注音，僅僅是注音，沒有任何意思。洋必須讀漢語音羊（yáng, 一ㄤˊ），不能直接用外語來讀。

洋（yáng, 一ㄤˊ）, "ocean", is a pictophonetic character. 氵 is the pictorial radical, or meaning element, representing 水「water」. On the other hand, 羊（yáng, 一ㄤˊ）serves as the phonetic radical, or sound element, that indicates its pronunciation. This sound element is specific to the Chinese language, thus 洋 can only be read in Chinese as 羊（yáng, 一ㄤˊ）, not in any other language. The meaning of 羊, "sheep", is not relevant in the character 洋, "ocean".

85

芳 (fāng, ㄈㄤ)
fragrant

芳是一個形聲字，艹 代表草的味道，方（fāng, ㄈㄤ）是漢語的注音，僅僅是注音，沒有任何意思，芳必須讀漢語音（fāng,ㄈㄤ），不能用外語來讀。

芳（fāng, ㄈㄤ），“fragrant”, is a pictophonetic character. 艹 is the pictorial radical, or meaning element, representing the smell of grass. On the other hand, 方（fāng, ㄈㄤ）serves as the phonetic radical that indicates its pronunciation, or sound element. This phonetic element is specific to the Chinese language, thus 芳 can only be read in Chinese as 方（fāng, ㄈㄤ）, not in any other language. The meaning of 方, “square”, is not relevant in the character 芳, “fragrant”.

86

因為假借字是借用漢語同音字的讀音來表達新的意思，所以必須讀漢語語音。

The sound of a phonetic loan character is derived from another character with the same pronunciation. That homophone is “loaned” to convey a new meaning. Since these homophones are specific to Chinese phonetics, phonetic loan characters can only be expressed orally in Chinese.

馬 (**mǎ, ㄇㄚˇ**) **horse.**

虎 (**hǔ, ㄏㄨˇ**) **tiger.**

馬和虎是象形字。

馬, “horse”, and 虎, “tiger”, are pictographic characters that can be directly read in any language.

馬馬虎虎是假借字，借用馬和虎的讀音，沒有借用馬和虎的意思。

When 馬 and 虎 are loaned to create new meanings, they become phonetic loan characters, no longer retaining their original meanings of “horse” and “tiger”. 馬馬虎虎（mǎ mǎ hǔ hǔ, ㄇㄚˇㄇㄚˇㄏㄨˇ ㄏㄨˇ）means “so-so” or “just passable”. These are phonetic loan characters, where only their sounds（not their meanings）are loaned. Because these sounds are specific to the Chinese language, they can only be read with Chinese pronunciation, not as “horse horse tiger tiger”in English.

對話

Dialogue

A: 您近來好嗎？

（nín jìn lái hǎo mā? ㄋㄧㄣˊ ㄐㄧㄣˋ ㄌㄞˊ ㄏㄠˇ ㄇㄚ?）

How are you getting on lately?

B: 馬馬虎虎。

（mǎ mǎ hǔ hǔ。ㄇㄚˇㄇㄚˇㄏㄨˇㄏㄨˇ。）

So far so good.

A: 您喜歡這本書嗎？

（nín xǐ huān zhè běn shū mā? ㄇㄚˇ ㄒㄧˇ ㄏㄨㄢ ㄓㄜˋ ㄅㄣˇ ㄕㄨ ㄇㄚ?）

Do you like this book?

B: 馬馬虎虎。

（mǎ mǎ hǔ hǔ。ㄇㄚˇㄇㄚˇㄏㄨˇㄏㄨˇ。）

Not so much.

A: 我的英語還可以嗎？

(wǒ dē yīng yǔ hái ké yǐ mā? ㄨㄛˇ ㄉㄜ ㄧㄥ ㄩˇ ㄏㄞˊ ㄎㄜˇ ㄧˇ ㄇㄚ?)

Is my English good?

B: 馬馬虎虎。

(mǎ mǎ hǔ hǔ。ㄇㄚˇㄇㄚˇㄏㄨˇㄏㄨˇ。)

So-so.

十 漢字的載體材料及其書體

Materials on which the Scripts were Written and the Script Styles

87

漢字依靠一定的載體材料來表現。歷史上不同載體材料的出現和變化，限定了漢字的書體及其演變。

Chinese characters relied on specific materials for their expression. As time passed, old materials fell into disuse and new ones emerged. This has influenced the styles of Chinese characters and their evolution.

漢字載體材料的歷史

History of materials used for Chinese characters

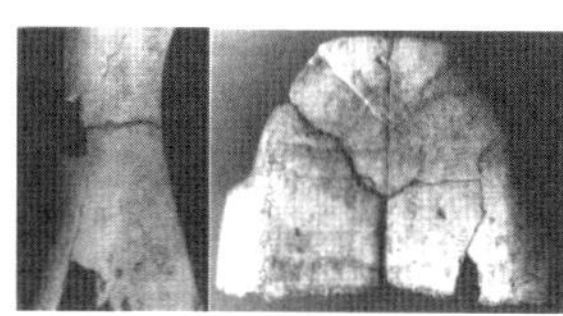

甲骨
Bone and tortoise shell

圖一
Picture 1

石碑
Stone tablets

圖二
Picture 2

青銅器
Bronze vessels

圖三
Picture 3

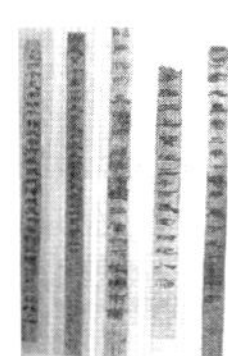

竹簡
Bamboo slips

圖四
Picture 4

木牘
Wooden slips

圖五
Picture 5

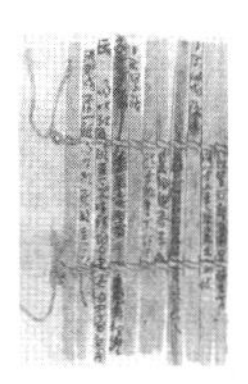

縑帛
Silk and textiles

圖六
Picture 6

紙
Paper

圖七
Picture 7

甲骨	殷代，西元前 16 至 11 世紀 Bone and tortoise shell The Yin Dynasty, 16th to 11th century BC.	如圖一 as Picture 1
石碑	起源於商代，西元前 11 世紀 Stone tablets Originated in the Shang Dynasty, 11th century BC	如圖二 as Picture 2
青銅器	起源於商代，西元前 11 世紀 Bronze vessels Originated in the Shang Dynasty, 11th century BC	如圖三 as Picture 3
竹簡	起源於商代，西元前 11 世紀 Bamboo slips Originated in the Shang Dynasty, 11th century BC	如圖四 as Picture 4
木牘	起源於商代，西元前 11 世紀 Wooden slips Originated in the Shang Dynasty, 11th century BC	如圖五 as Picture 5
縑帛	起源於春秋時代，西元前 770 年 Silk and textiles Originated in the Spring and Autumn Period, 770 BC	如圖六 as Picture 6
紙	發明於東漢時代，西元 63-121 年 Paper Invented in the Eastern Han Dynasty, 63 – 121 AD	如圖七 as Picture 7

88

漢字書體的演變歷程

The evolution of Chinese character styles

漢字 拼音 國語注音 英語 Characters *Pinyin* Mandarin Phonetic symbol English	甲骨文 (殷) 西元前 16 至 11 世紀 Oracle bone script Yin Dynasty 16th to 11th century BC	金文 (商、周) 西元前 1066 至 256 年 Bronze script Shang & Zhou Dynasties 1066 to 256 BC	篆書 (秦) 始於西元前 221 年 Seal scripts Qin Dynasty Starting in 221 BC	隸書 (秦、漢) 西元前 221 年至西元 220 年 Clerical script Qin and Han Dynasties 221 BC to 220 AD
 耳 ěr ㄦˇ ear				
 口 kǒu ㄎㄡˇ mouth				
 目 mù ㄇㄨˋ eye				
 身 shēn ㄕㄣ body				

	楷書 （漢、魏、晉） 西元 202 至 420 年 Regular script Han, Wei and Jin Dynasties 202-420 AD	草書 （漢末） 西元 202 至 220 年 Cursive script Late Han Dynasty 202-220 AD	行書 （漢末） 西元 202 至 220 年 Running script Late Han Dynasty 202-220 AD	宋體 （宋朝） 西元 420 至 1279 年 Song typeface Song Dynasty 420-1279 AD
	耳	耳	耳	耳
	口	口	口	口
	目	目	目	目
	身	身	身	身

衣 yī ㄧ clothes					
巾 jīn ㄐㄧㄣ towel					
床 Chuáng ㄔㄨㄤˊ bed					
門 mén ㄇㄣˊ door					
宮 gōng ㄍㄨㄥ palace					
高 gāo ㄍㄠ high					
鼎 dǐng ㄉㄧㄥˇ tripod					

	衣	衣	衣	衣
	巾	巾	巾	巾
	牀	床	床	床
	門	門	门	門 (门)
	宮	宮	宮	宮
	高	高	高	高
	鼎	鼎	鼎	鼎

車 chē ㄕㄣ carriage					
舟 zhōu ㄓㄡ boat					
林 lín ㄌㄧㄣˊ forest					
絲 sī ㄙ silk					
米 mǐ ㄇㄧˇ rice					
雨 yǔ ㄩˇ rain					
羽 yǔ ㄩˇ feather					

	車	車	車	車(车)
	舟	舟	舟	舟
	林	林	林	林
	絲	絲	絲	絲(丝)
	米	米	米	米
	雨	雨	雨	雨
	羽	羽	羽	羽

89

從十二生肖書體的演變過程，看各種書體的特點和關係。

From the evolution of the 12 Chinese Zodiac character styles, we can observe the characteristics and relationships of various scripts.

甲骨文（十二生肖）

Oracle bone scripts of the 12 Chinese Zodiac

	(鼠 shǔ, ㄕㄨˇ)		(牛 niú, ㄋㄧㄡˊ)		(虎 hǔ, ㄏㄨˇ)
	rat		cow		tiger
	(兔 tù, ㄊㄨˋ)		(龍 lóng, ㄌㄨㄥˊ)		(蛇 shé, ㄕㄜˊ)
	rabbit		dragon		snake
	(馬 mǎ, ㄇㄚˇ)		(羊 yáng, ㄧㄤˊ)		(猴 hóu, ㄏㄡˊ)
	horse		goat		monkey
	(雞 jī, ㄐㄧ)		(狗 gǒu, ㄍㄡˇ)		(豬 zhū, ㄓㄨ)
	rooster		dog		pig

甲骨文最接近物象的形狀。甲骨文已經不再使用。人們只用它作書法裝飾之用。

The oracle bone script is closest to the real shapes of objects. It is no longer in regular use; it is now only used for decorative purposes in calligraphy.

金文（十二生肖）

Bronze scripts of the 12 Chinese Zodiac

	(鼠) rat		(牛) cow		(虎) tiger		(兔) rabbit
	(龍) dragon		(蛇) snake		(馬) horse		(羊) goat
	(猴) monkey		(雞) rooster		(狗) dog		(豬) pig

金文接近物象的形狀，同時開始變得比較方形。金文已經不再使用。人們只用它作書法裝飾之用。

The Bronze script is also close to the shapes of objects, while starting to become squarer in form. It is no longer in regular use; it is now only used for decorative purposes in calligraphy.

篆書（十二生肖）

Seal scripts of the 12 Chinese Zodiac

	(鼠) rat		(牛) cow		(虎) tiger		(兔) rabbit
	(龍) dragon		(蛇) snake		(馬) horse		(羊) goat
	(猴) monkey		(雞) rooster		(狗) dog		(豬) pig

篆書一直用在書法和篆刻上。

The Seal script has always been used in calligraphy and seal carving.

隸書（十二生肖）

Clerical scripts of the 12 Chinese Zodiac

鼠	（鼠） rat	牛	（牛） cow	虎	（虎） tiger	兔	（兔） rabbit
龍	（龍） dragon	蛇	（蛇） snake	馬	（馬） horse	羊	（羊） goat
猴	（猴） monkey	雞	（雞） rooster	犬	（狗） dog	豕	（豬） pig

隸書……是秦、漢朝官員使用的文字，是漢字脱離象形的分水嶺。自隸書以後的書體不再是象形的了，所以人們學習識字時，一般不再去了解字的原來象形是怎樣的。

The Clerical script was used by officials during the Qin and Han dynasties（206 BC. - 220 AD）and marks a turning point in the evolution of Chinese characters away from pictographs. After the introduction of clerical script, the later script styles no longer relied on pictographic forms. Thus, when learning to read and write, people generally do not concern themselves with how the original pictographs looked.

楷書（十二生肖）

Regular scripts of the 12 Chinese zodiac

鼠	（鼠） rat	牛	（牛） cow	虎	（虎） tiger	兔	（兔） rabbit
龍	（龍） dragon	蛇	（蛇） snake	馬	（馬） horse	羊	（羊） goat
猴	（猴） monkey	雞	（雞） rooster	犬	（狗） dog	豕	（豬） pig

楷書筆劃比隸書簡易。

The strokes of Regular script are simpler than those of Clerical script.

草書（十二生肖）

Cursive scripts of the 12 Chinese zodiac

鼠	（鼠） rat	牛	（牛） cow	虎	（虎） tiger	兔	（兔） rabbit
龍	（龍） dragon	蛇	（蛇） snake	馬	（馬） horse	羊	（羊） goat
猴	（猴） monkey	雞	（雞） rooster	犬	（狗） dog	豕	（豬） pig

草書是快速手寫體。

The Cursive script is used in fast handwriting.

行書（十二生肖）

Running scripts of the 12 Chinese zodiac

鼠	（鼠） rat	牛	（牛） cow	虎	（虎） tiger	兔	（兔） rabbit
龍	（龍） dragon	蛇	（蛇） snake	馬	（馬） horse	羊	（羊） goat
猴	（猴） monkey	雞	（雞） rooster	犬	（狗） dog	豕	（豬） pig

行書比楷書隨意和容易寫。

The Running script is more casual and easier to write than Regular script.

楷書、草書、行書都是當前流行的手寫體。

The Regular script, Cursive script and Running script are all popular handwriting styles today.

宋體字（十二生肖）

Song typeface of the 12 Chinese zodiac

鼠	（鼠） rat	牛	（牛） cow	虎	（虎） tiger	兔	（兔） rabbit
龍	（龍） dragon	蛇	（蛇） snake	馬	（馬） horse	羊	（羊） goat
猴	（猴） monkey	雞	（雞） rooster	狗	（狗） dog	豬	（豬） pig

宋體字是宋朝（西元 960 年至 1279 年）發明的漢字印刷字體。

The Song typeface is a printed Chinese font that was invented during the Song Dynasty（960-1279 AD）.

十一 為什麼漢字是方塊形的？

Why are Chinese Characters Square-Shaped

90

周朝燕侯鼎銘文（前 1046-256 年）

Zhou dynasty（1046 to 256 BC）Bronze scripts.

古人在製造銅器銘文時，要先在銅器上面劃好方形框線，然後在方框中寫入銘文的字，方塊字是如此形成的。古人在方框中，建造了端正、和諧、美觀的不同形體的漢字。

When the ancient Chinese were making inscriptions on bronze vessels, they would first draw square outlines on the surface of the bronze, then write the characters within the frames. This is how square characters were formed. It is inside these very frames that ancient artisans created upright, harmonious, and beautiful variations of Chinese characters.

91

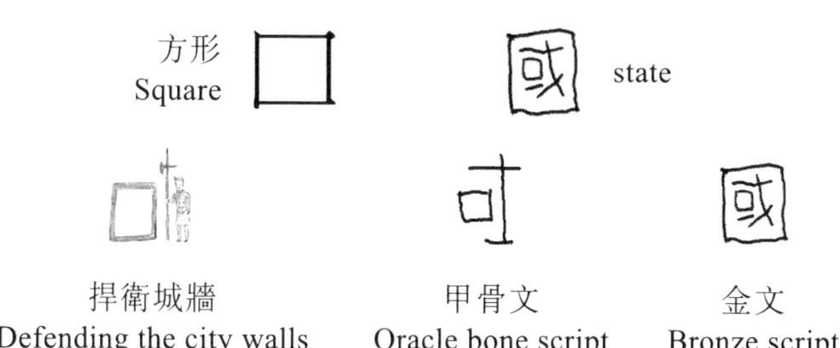

捍衛城牆
Defending the city walls

甲骨文
Oracle bone script

金文
Bronze script

「國」字的金文國是將甲骨文可 修改為方形。口是城牆，丅是保衛城牆的武器。

國（guó, ㄍㄨㄛˊ），“state” . Its Bronze script 國 is constructed by modifying its oracle bone script 可 into a square character. 口 is the city wall and 丅 is a weapon used for defending the city.

92

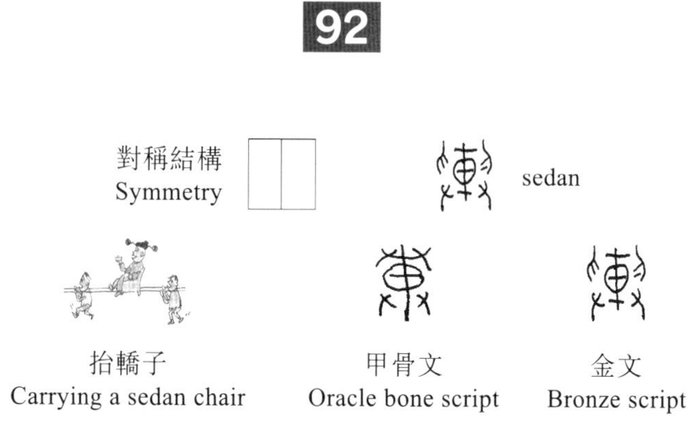

抬轎子
Carrying a sedan chair

甲骨文
Oracle bone script

金文
Bronze script

「輿」的金文，幾隻手抬著轎子。輿夫們的議論叫做「輿論」，是信得過的。今天沒有輿夫了，代之有官老爺的司機，司機們的議論也最能代表社會輿論，也是信得過的，因為他們經常聽到官老爺們私底下交談的話都是真話，是可靠的消息來源，不像官老爺在正式場合所說的話不一定是真話。

「輿」(yú, ㄩˊ), “sedan”. Its Bronze script shows several hands carrying a sedan chair. The discussions of the sedan chair bearers are collectively known as “public opinion” and are considered credible. Nowadays there are no more bearers; instead, officials have their own private drivers. Just like their ancient counterparts, these private drivers’ discussions also best represent social public opinion which is trustworthy. This is because they often overhear the private conversations of their masters, which are the most reliable source of information, as opposed to what their masters might say in public, which is not always truthful.

93

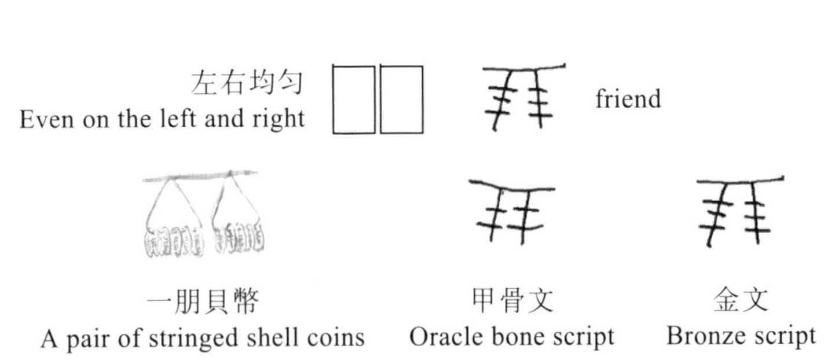

「朋」的金文是一對貝幣，貝幣是最古老的貨幣。由於唸 péng，ㄆㄥˊ音，所以被借來當作「朋友」的「朋」字。

朋（péng, ㄆㄥˊ）in Bronze script is a pair of stringed shell coins, the oldest currency. is pronounced péng, ㄆㄥˊ, so（朋）is loaned to express 朋友（péng yǒu, ㄆㄥˊ ㄧㄡˇ）, “friend”.

94

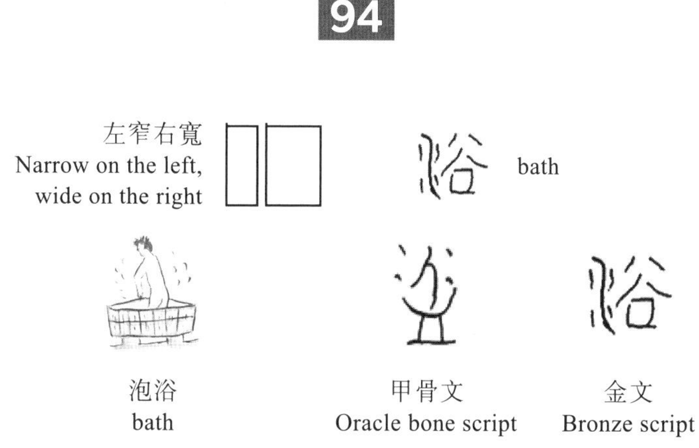

泡浴 bath　甲骨文 Oracle bone script　金文 Bronze script

「浴」的金文是將甲骨文修改為方塊形。

浴（yù, ㄩˋ），“bath”. Its Bronze script is constructed by modifying its Oracle Bone script into a square.

95

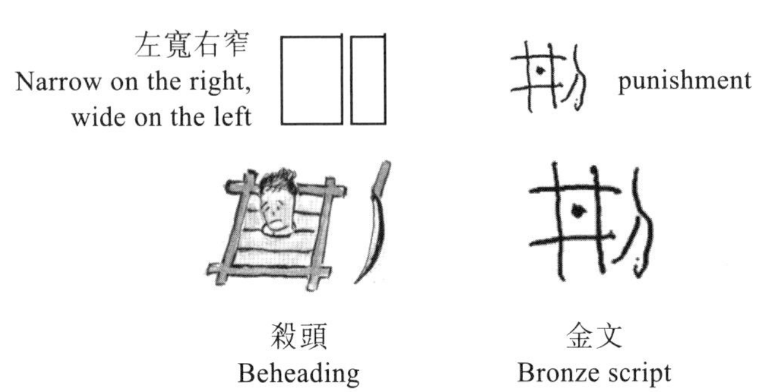

「刑」字的金文，一個披枷帶鎖的罪人被砍頭。

刑（xíng，ㄒㄧㄥˊ），"punishment". Its Bronze script shows the beheading of a prisoner in chains and shackles.

96

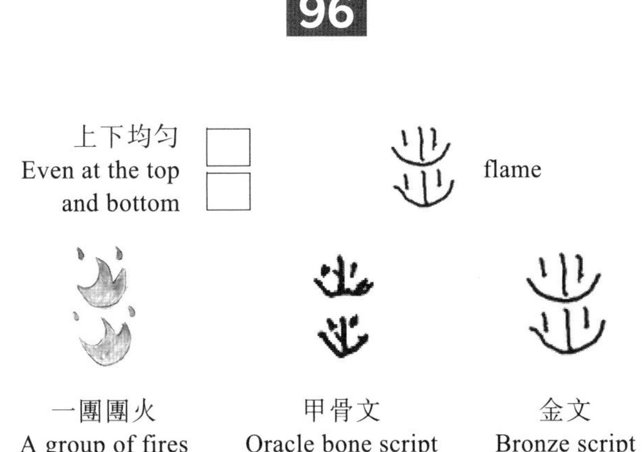

「炎」的金文　　，一團團火。

炎（yàn, ㄧㄢˋ），“flame”. Its Bronze script shows clusters of flames.

97

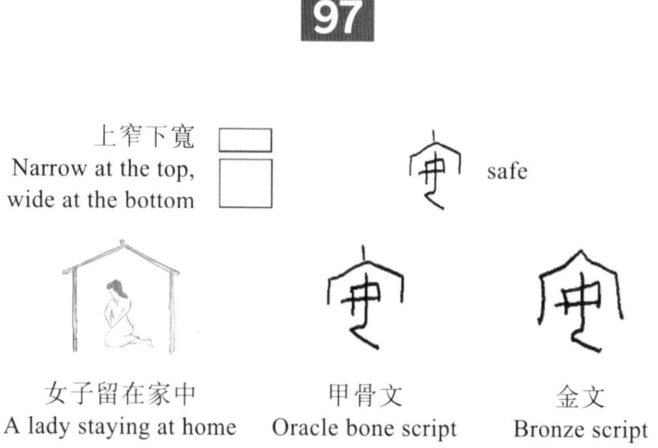

「安」的金文　　，女子留在家中是安全的。

安（ān, ㄢ），“safe”. Its Bronze script　　shows a lady staying at home, implying her safety is ensured.

98

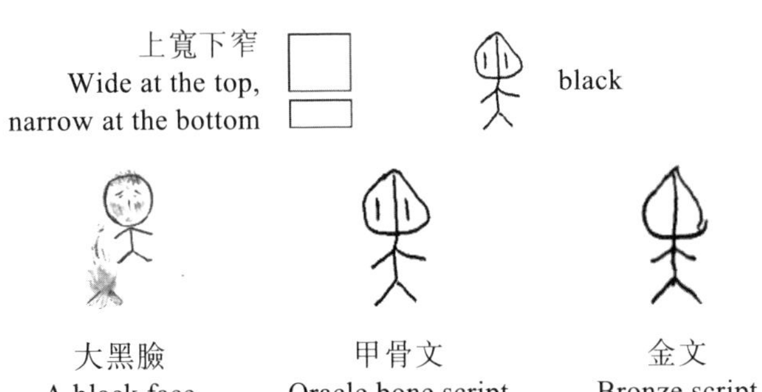

「黑」字的金文 ，一個被熏黑的臉。

黑（hēi, ㄏㄟ），“black”. Its Bronze script is a face blackened by smoke.

99

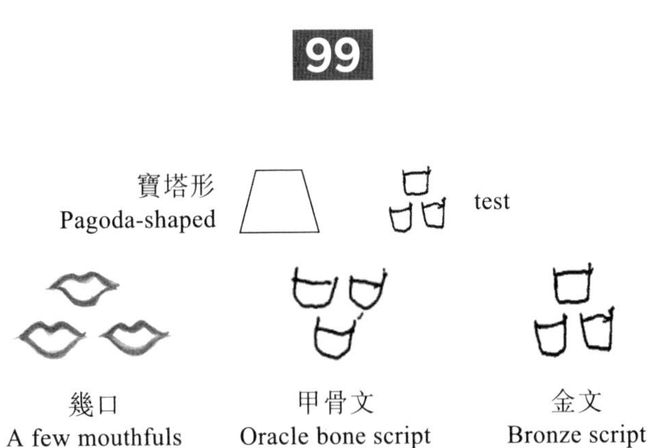

「品」的金文 品 ，嘗嘗數口。

品（pǐn, ㄆㄧㄣˇ）, “test”. Its Bronze script 品 means “try a few mouthfuls”.

十二 文房四寶？

Four Treasures of the Study

100

「筆、墨、硯、紙」為文房四寶，毛筆最為重要，沒有毛筆就沒有中國書法和國畫。

Brush, ink, inkstone, and paper are known as “Four Treasures of the Study”. The brush is the most important, without which there would be no Chinese calligraphy and traditional paintings.

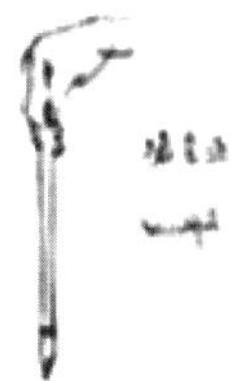

要寫好毛筆字，首先握筆要正確。

To write Chinese calligraphy well, one must first hold the brush properly.

102

最普遍使用的標準的毛筆握筆方法

The most commonly used standard method for holding a brush

五指執筆法（wǔ zhǐ zhí bǐ fǎ，ㄨˇ ㄓˇ ㄓˊ ㄅㄧˇ ㄈㄚˇ）

Wu Zhi Zhi Bi Fa（The five-finger grip method）

103

由於筆桿的粗細不同，書法不同，字體的大小不同，將字寫上的地方不同，寫字人的姿勢不同，就需要有另外幾種不同的握筆方法。

Due to differences in brush thickness, calligraphy styles, font sizes, the surface on which the characters are written, and the writer's posture, there are several other methods of holding a Chinese brush.

幾種常用的握筆法

Popular methods of holding a Chinese writing brush

撚管法（niǎn guǎn fǎ, ㄋㄧㄢˇ ㄍㄨㄢˇ ㄈㄚˇ） Nian Guan Fa, the method of "twisting".	
撥鐙法（bō dèng fǎ, ㄅㄛ ㄉㄥˋ ㄈㄚˇ） Bo Deng Fa, the method of "picking".	
撮管法（cuō guǎn fǎ,ㄘㄨㄛ ㄍㄨㄢˇ ㄈㄚˇ） Cuo Guan Fa, the method of "pinching".	
雙鈎法（shuāng gōu fǎ, ㄕㄨㄤ ㄍㄡ ㄈㄚˇ） Shuang Gou Fa, the method of "double hooking".	

單鈎法（dān gōu fǎ, ㄉㄢ ㄍㄡ ㄈㄚˇ） Dan Gou Fa, the method of “single hooking”.	
握管法（wò guǎn fǎ, ㄨㄛˋㄍㄡ ㄈㄚˇ） Wo Guan Fa, the method of “grasping”.	

書寫時的不同姿態

Different postures while writing:

坐姿寫 Writing while sitting	
跪姿寫 Writing while kneeling	
站姿寫 Writing while standing	

104

練習

Exercise

楷書是最廣泛使用的手寫體。

Regular script is the most widely used handwriting style.

龍（lóng , ㄌㄨㄥˊ）dragon

蛇（shé, ㄕㄜˊ）snake

馬（mǎ, ㄇㄚˇ）horse

羊（yáng, 一ㄤˊ）goat

猴（hóu, ㄏㄡˊ）monkey

鷄 （jī, ㄐㄧ） chicken

鷄	鷄	鷄	鷄	鷄	鷄	鷄	鷄	鷄	鷄
鷄	鷄	鷄	鷄	鷄	鷄	鷄	鷄	鷄	鷄
鷄									

狗 （gǒu, ㄍㄡˇ） dog

狗	狗	狗	狗	狗	狗	狗	狗		

豬 （zhū, ㄓㄨ） pig

豬	豬	豬	豬	豬	豬	豬	豬	豬	豬
豬	豬	豬	豬	豬					

十三 如何寫字

How to Write Chinese Characters

105

楷書的八種筆劃

The eight strokes of Regular script

筆劃名稱 stroke name	筆劃 stroke	字例 character examples	英譯 meaning
(1) 點 (diǎn, ㄉㄧㄢˇ) dot	丶	黑 心 冬	黑 black, 心 heart, 冬 winter
(2) 橫 (héng, ㄏㄥˊ) cross	一	三 面 哥	三 three, 面 face, 哥 brother
(3) 豎 (shù, ㄕˋ) vertical	丨	上 半 山	上 up, 半 half, 山 mountain

(4) 勾 （gōu, ㄍㄡ） hook	亅	小 食 把	小 small, 食 food, 把 hold
(5) 挑 （tiāo, ㄊㄧㄠ） rising	㇀	地 打 活	地 earth, 打 beat, 活 live
(6) （wān, ㄨㄢ） turning	㇆	包 弓 老	包 pack, 弓 bow, 老 old
(7) 撇 （piē, ㄆㄧㄝ） left-falling	㇒	八 人 厂	八 eight, 人 human, 厂 factory
(8) 捺 （nà, ㄋㄚˋ） right-falling	㇏	大 木 走	大 big, 木 wood, 走 walk

106

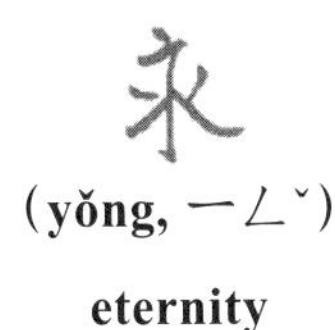

(yǒng, ㄩㄥˇ)

eternity

永字含有楷書的八種筆劃，故稱「永字八法」。

The character 永（yǒng, ㄩㄥˇ）, “eternity”, contains the eight strokes of Regular script, thus referred to as the “Method of the Eight Strokes”.

Brush writing

點 Dot	橫 Cross	豎 Vertical	勾 Hook	挑 Rising	彎 Turning	撇 Left falling	捺 Right falling

Pen writing

點 Dot	橫 Cross	豎 Vertical	勾 Hook	挑 Rising	彎 Turning	撇 Left falling	捺 Right falling

練習

Exercise

一（yī, 一） one

二（èr, ㄦˋ） two

三（sān, ㄙㄢ） three

四（sì, ㄙˋ） four

五（wǔ, ㄨˇ） five

六（liù, ㄌㄧㄡˋ） six

七（qī, ㄑㄧ） seven

八（bā, ㄅㄚ） eight

九（jiǔ, ㄐㄧㄡˇ） nine

十（shí, ㄕˊ） ten

零（líng, ㄌㄧㄥˊ） zero

我（wǒ, ㄨㄛˇ） I, me

你（nǐ, ㄋㄧˇ） you

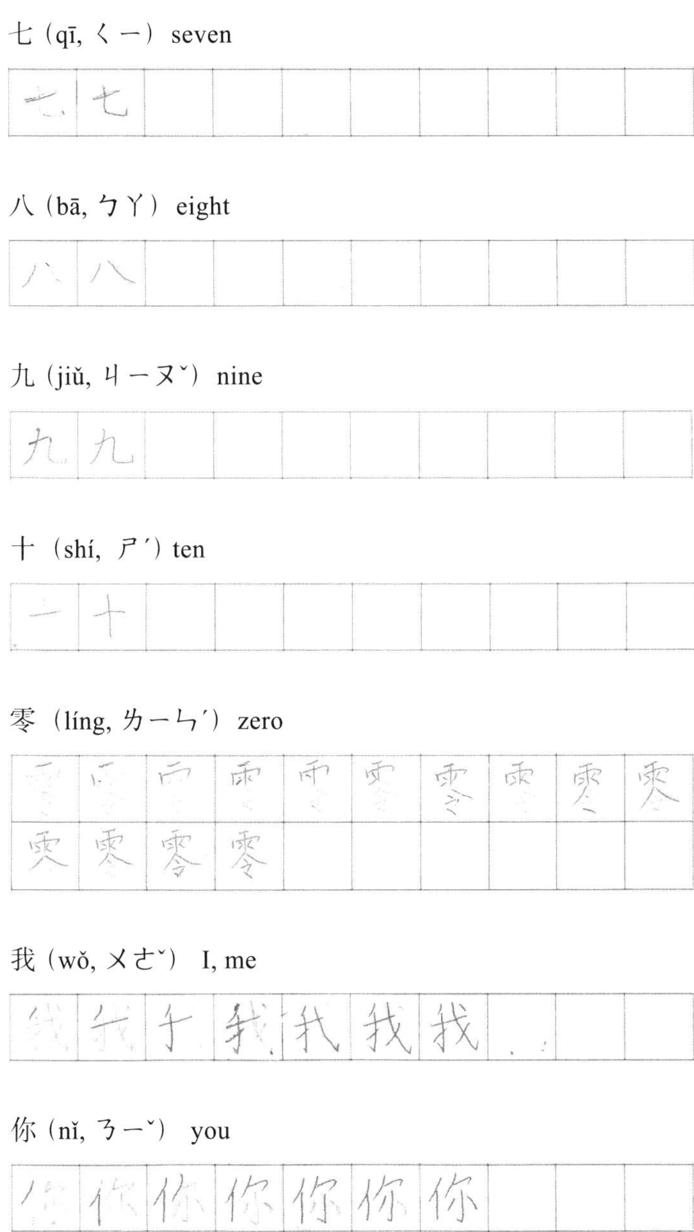

妳（nǐ, ㄋㄧˇ）you（female）

他（tā, ㄊㄚ）he, him

她（tā, ㄊㄚ）she, her

男（nān, ㄋㄢ）male

女（nǚ, ㄋㄩˇ）female

十四 外國人的老大難——認字

To Recognize Chinese Characters is a "Hard Nut to Crack" for Foreigners

108

一個漢字是一幅圖畫，所以有些外國人認為漢字不是寫出來，而是畫出來的。他們習慣於拼寫字母，感到漢字難記難寫。他們雖然能說一口流利的漢語，卻不會認字和寫字，始終領略不到漢字的迷人藝術。

A Chinese character is like a picture, so some foreigners believe that Chinese characters are not written but drawn. They are accustomed to spelling and find Chinese characters difficult to remember and write. Although they may speak fluent Chinese, they cannot recognize or write characters, and therefore never fully appreciate the charm of Chinese characters.

109

嚴格而言，要記好漢字沒有捷徑，唯有多看多寫。當你積累一定數量的漢字，自然地觸類旁通。

Strictly speaking, there is no shortcut to memorizing Chinese characters; you can only build a strong vocabulary by reading and writing them diligently. Once you have accumulated a certain number of characters, you will naturally start to make connections between them.

前面談及的「六書」歸納了漢字的構成和使用方式的六條例，是幫助我們認字的方法。下面舉三個例子：

As previously mentioned, 六書（Liu Shu）, the "Six Writing Forms", summarize six rules for the composition and usage of Chinese characters, helping us recognize them. Here are three examples:

(1)

表示讀音的部首「馬」(mǎ，ㄇㄚˇ)

The sound radical 馬（mǎ，ㄇㄚˇ）"horse"

有關聯讀音的部首能幫助你記憶一些字。例如「馬、碼、媽、螞、罵」這些字都與「馬」的讀音有關。

The sound radicals that share the same pronunciations can help you remember certain characters. For example, the characters 馬（mǎ，ㄇㄚˇ）"horse", 碼（mǎ，ㄇㄚˇ）"code", 媽（mā，ㄇㄚ）"mother", 螞（mǎ，ㄇㄚˇ）"ant", and 罵（mà，ㄇㄚˋ）"scold" all contain the sound radical 馬（mǎ，ㄇㄚˇ）and share the same pronunciation.

(2)

表示象形的部首「宀」(室)

The graphic radical 宀 "room"

有關聯象形的部首能幫助你記憶一些字，例如「家、寶、宮、官、空、穴、安、寵、賓、室」這些字都與宀部首有關。

The graphic radicals which share the same pictographs may help you recognize some characters，for example, 家（jiā, ㄐㄧㄚ）"home" , 寶（bǎo, ㄅㄠˇ）"treasure", 宮（gōng, ㄍㄨㄥ）"palace", 官（guān, ㄍㄨㄢ）"official", 空（kōng, ㄎㄨㄥ）"empty", 穴（xué, ㄒㄩㄝˊ）"hole", 安（ān, ㄢ）"peace", 寵（chǒng , ㄔㄨㄥˇ）"pet", 賓（bīn, ㄅㄧㄣ）"guest", and 室（shì, ㄕˋ）"room" all contain the graphic radical 宀 "room", and share a connection through the same pictograph.

(3)

表示動作的部首「扌」(手)

The action radical 扌 "hand"

有關聯動作的部首能幫助你記憶一些字，例如「打、扛、抓、拆、挖、揮、換」這些字都與扌（手）部首有關。

The action radicals may help you recognize some characters, for example, 打（dǎ, ㄉㄚˇ）"beat", 扛（káng, ㄎㄤˊ）"carry", 抓（zhuā, ㄓㄨㄚ）"grab", 拆（chāi, ㄔㄞ）"dismantle", 挖（wā, ㄨㄚ）"dig", 揮（huī, ㄏㄨㄟ）"wave", and 換（huàn, ㄏㄨㄢˋ）"change" all contain the action radical 扌 "hand". These characters all mean actions that are made by hands.

十五 漢字的書寫排列
Vertical and Horizontal Arrangements of Chinese Characters

110

一個漢字一個單位，所以書寫排列靈活，可以由右到左縱向排列，也可以從左到右橫向排列。

As each Chinese character is an individual unit, the writing arrangement is flexible. Characters can be arranged vertically from right to left or horizontally from left to right.

111

傳統漢字的書寫排列是由右向左縱向排列。這是古代簡牘方便書寫的緣故。

Traditionally, Chinese characters are arranged vertically from right to left, because this orientation was convenient for writing on ancient bamboo and wooden slips.

人之初
性本善

人之初，

(rén zhī chū，

ㄖㄣˊㄓ ㄔㄨ，)

Man at birth,

性本善。

(xìng běn shàn。

ㄒㄧㄥˋ ㄅㄣˇ ㄕㄢˋ 。)

is fundamentally good in nature.

112

在清代末年 1861 至 1895 年的洋務運動中，受西方文字排列的影響，漢字書寫才出現了由左向右的橫向排列。

During the late Qing Dynasty's Westernization Movement from 1861 to 1895, Chinese writing adopted horizontal arrangement from left to right, like that of Western alphabets.

人 之 初，

性 本 善。

十六 漢字的數量

The Quantity of Chinese Characters

113

經過幾千年的艱苦積累，現有數萬個漢字。文字在積累的過程中不斷地增加一些字和淘汰一些字，所以究竟有過多少字，至今沒有準確的統計。

After thousands of years of gradual accumulation, there are now tens of thousands of Chinese characters. Throughout this process, new characters came into being while others were discarded, so the exact total of all characters over time remains unknown.

114

已經發現的甲骨文單字大約有 4000 多個。

As of now there are more than 4000 unearthed Oracle Bone scripts.

115

籀文（大篆）大約有 3000 個。

As of now there are about 3000 Zhouwen Seal scripts（Great Seal scripts）.

116

小篆大約有 3300 個。

As of now there are about 3300 Small Seal scripts.

117

掌握約 2500 至 3500 個常用字，就能閱讀報紙和書刊，因為字可以組成許多詞，例如由「學」與「問」組成「學問」；「飛」與「機」組成「飛機」等等。

By mastering about 2,500 to 3,500 commonly used characters, one can read newspapers and publications. This is because two or more single characters can form new words and phrases; for example, 學（xué，ㄒㄩㄝˊ）means "study" and 問（wèn，ㄨㄣˋ）means "ask". They combine to form 學問 "knowledge"which is related to 學 "theory" and 問 "problem". Let's also note that 學問 "knowledge" is gained from 學（xué，ㄒㄩㄝˊ）"studying" and 問（wèn，ㄨㄣˋ）"asking".

飛機（fēi jī, ㄈㄟ ㄐㄧ）airplane

飛（fēi, ㄈㄟ）, meaning “fly”, and 機（jī, ㄐㄧ）, meaning “machine”, combine to form 飛機 , which translates to “airplane ”. The word-for-word translation of 飛機 as “flying machine” also makes sense.

十七 從鈔票上的漢字說起

Chinese Characters on Banknotes

118

人民幣

RMB（Ren Min Bi）

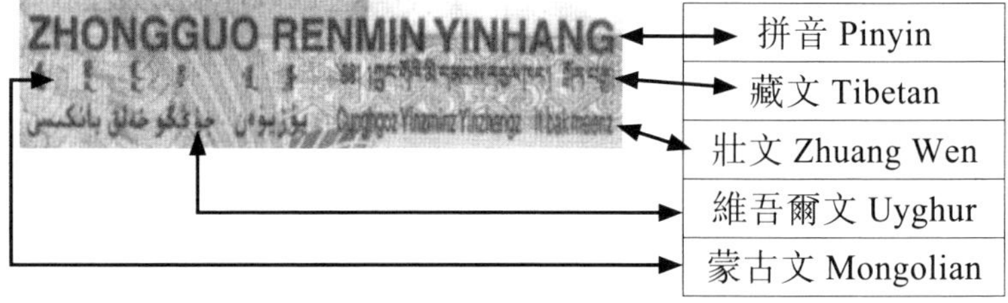

在人民幣鈔票上面有中文拼音、漢文、蒙古文、藏文、維吾爾文和壯文等。《中華人民共和國國家通用語言文字法》界定「國家通用語言文字是普通話和規範漢字」，同時十分重視保護少數民族語言文字。

Renminbi（RMB） banknotes feature various characters, including pinyin, Chinese characters, Mongolian, Tibetan, Uyghur, and Zhuang. The "Law of the People's Republic of China on the National Common Language" defines the national common language and script as Standard Putonghua and standardized Chinese characters, while also placing great emphasis on the protection of minority languages and scripts.

簡化字

Simplified characters

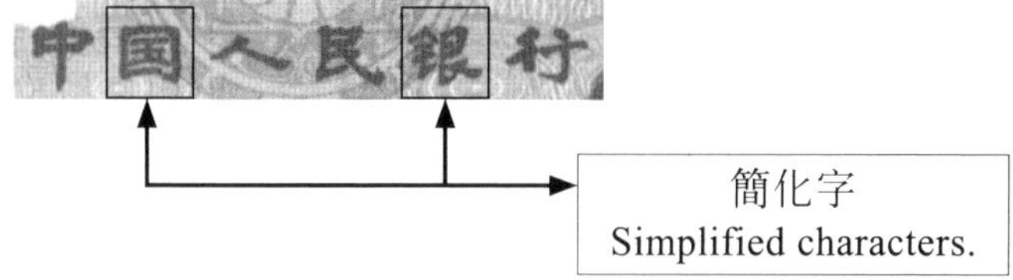

中国人民银行（**zhōngguǒ rénmín yínháng**
ㄓㄨㄥ ㄍㄛˊ ㄖㄣˊㄇㄧㄣˊ ㄧㄣˊㄏㄤˊ）

People's Bank of China.

国、银分別是國、銀的簡化字。

国（guó, ㄍ ㄛˊ）, "country", and 银（yín, ㄧㄣˊ）, "silver", are the simplified forms of 國 and 銀 respectively。

119

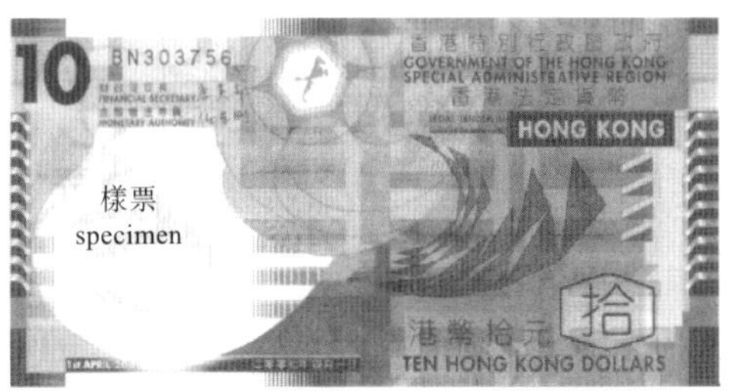

港幣

HKD（Hong Kong Dollar）

正體字

Traditional characters

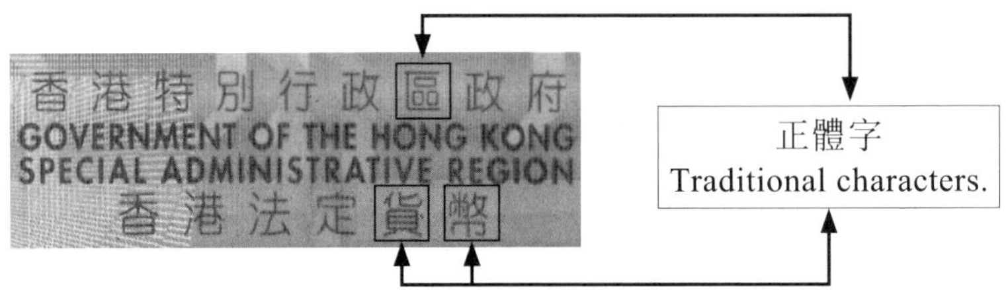

香港特別行政區政府

（xiāng gǎng tèbié xíng zhèng qū zhèng fǔ

ㄒㄧㄤ ㄍㄤˇ ㄊㄜˋㄅㄧㄝˊ ㄒㄧㄥˊㄓㄥˋㄑㄩ ㄓㄥˋㄈㄨˇ）

GOVERNMENT OF THE HONG KONG SPECIAL ADMINISTRATIVE REGION

香港法定貨幣

（xiāng gǎng fǎ dìng huò bì）

ㄒㄧㄤㄍㄤˇ ㄈㄚˇㄉㄧㄥˋ ㄏㄨㄛˋㄅㄧˋ)

Legal Tender in Hong Kong

區、貨、幣 分別是区、货、币的正體字。

區（qū, ㄑㄩ）, “region”, 貨（huò , ㄏㄨㄛˋ）, “goods”, and 幣（bì , ㄅㄧˋ）, “currency”, are the traditional forms of 区 , 货 and 币 respectively.

120

澳門幣

MOP（Macau Pataca）

正體字

Traditional characters

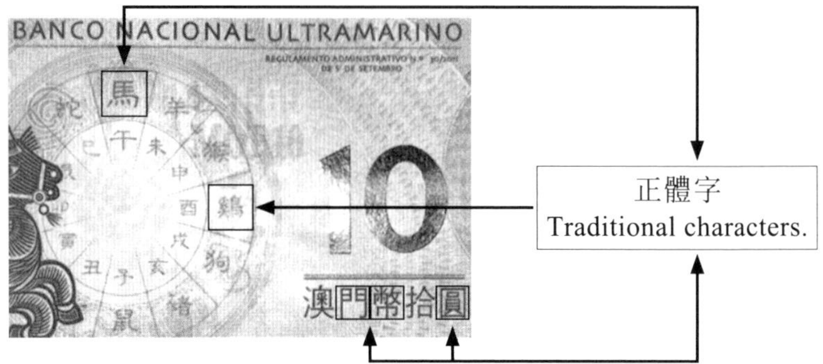

馬、雞、門、幣、圓 分別是马、鸡、门、币、元的正體字。

馬（mǎ,ㄇㄚˇ）“horse”, 雞（jī,ㄐㄧ）“chicken”, 門（mén, ㄇㄣˊ）“door”, 幣（bì, ㄅㄧˋ）“currency”, and 圓（yuan, ㄩㄢˊ）, “dollar”, are the traditional forms of 马 , 鸡, 门 , 币 and 元 respectively.

121

從鈔票上的漢字可以看到，中國官方使用簡化字，而台灣、香港和澳門地區的官方使用正體字。

From the Chinese characters on banknotes, it is evident that Simplified characters are officially adopted in mainland China, while Traditional characters are used officially in Taiwan, Hong Kong and Macao.

但是在民間，簡化字和正體字都一起使用。

However, in daily life, both Simplified and Traditional characters are used together.

十八 繁體字與簡化字的爭論

The Debate over Complex and Simplified Characters

122

二十世紀五十年代，中國大陸開展文字改革運動，將二千多個常用字改為簡化字，隨即引起繁體字與簡化字的爭論，這個爭論已經有將近七十年之久，而且還會繼續下去。

In the 1950s, a movement to reform the written language was initiated in mainland China, simplifying more than 2000 daily used characters. This immediately sparked a debate between complex and simplified characters, a discussion that has lasted nearly seventy years and is likely to continue.

123

被簡化之前的常用字又叫做「繁體字」，與其「簡化字」相對應。

顧名思義，簡化字是將繁體字簡化。但是簡體字和簡化字是不同的。幾千年來有一部分漢字以簡體字和繁體字的形式出現，它們沒有「簡化」和「被簡化」的關係，它們同時使用，從無矛盾。例如，簡體字「云」和「气」就早於繁體字「雲」和「氣」，怎麼能說「云」和「气」分別是「雲」和「氣」的簡化字呢？

顯然，簡體字和簡化字不同，就不應該把簡體字和簡化字都英譯成 simplified characters，而應該分別翻譯為簡體字 simple characters 和簡化字 simplified characters。

繁體字與簡體字有史以來並存，各有優缺點。向來人們都是自行選擇怎樣使用繁體字與簡體字。政治上的爭執實在是無知，因為使用同一種字體的人不一定持有相同的政見。

有一些字既不屬於簡化字（或簡體字），也不屬於繁體字，例如「朋友」，它們是傳承字。

為什麼繁體字而不是簡體字被稱為正體字呢？因為《康熙字典》所錄的是繁體字和傳承字，是清政府官方使用的標準字體。

The commonly used characters 常用字（cháng yòng zì, ㄔㄤˊ ㄩㄥˋ ㄗˋ）before being simplified are known as 繁體字（fán tǐ zì, ㄈㄢˊ ㄊㄧˇ ㄗˋ）, “complex characters”, which correspond to their simplified counterparts 簡化字（jiǎn huà zì, ㄐㄧㄢˇ ㄏㄨㄚˋ ㄗˋ）, “simplified characters”.

As the name suggests, simplified characters are created by “simplifying”complex characters. However, we should make a distinction between 簡體字（jiǎn tǐ zì, ㄐㄧㄢˇ ㄊㄧˇ ㄗˋ）, “simple characters”, and 簡化字（jiǎn huà zì, ㄐㄧㄢˇ ㄏㄨㄚˋ ㄗˋ）, “simplified characters”. For thousands of years, some Chinese characters have appeared in both simple and complex forms, and there is no relationship of "simplification" or "being simplified" between them; they are used simultaneously without contradiction. For example, the simple characters 云（yún）, "cloud", and 气（qì）, "air", appeared before the complex characters 雲（yún）and 氣（qì）, so it cannot be said that 云 and 气 are the simplified forms of 雲 and 氣 , respectively.

Obviously, 簡體字 , "simple characters", are different from 簡化字 , "simplified characters". Therefore, we should not translate both as "simplified characters" in English. Instead, they should be translated as "simple characters"and "simplified characters", respectively.

Throughout history, complex characters and simple characters have coexisted, each with its own strengths and weaknesses. Using complex or simple characters is entirely a matter of personal choice. Political disputes over this matter are truly ignorant, as using the same characters does not necessarily mean sharing the same political views.

Some characters are neither simplified（or simple）characters nor complex characters, such as the word 朋友 , "friend". These are known as inherited characters.

Why are complex characters, but not simple characters, referred to as "Traditional characters"（正體字）? This is because the Kangxi Dictionary recorded Traditional and inherited characters, which were the standard scripts officially used by the Qing government.

124

有一些簡化字把筆劃少的字當作筆劃多的同音異義字的簡化字，造成字義混淆。例如，把「面」當作「麵」的簡化字，「她在下面」這個句子是指「她在做麵食」，還是「她在下方位置」呢？又如把「后」當作「後」的簡化字，「皇后有幾個隨從」到底是「在皇帝的後面有幾個隨從」還是「皇帝的妻子有幾個隨從」呢？

Some simplified characters use characters with fewer strokes as simplified forms of homophones with more strokes, leading to confusion in meaning. For example, 面（miàn, ㄇㄧㄢˋ）, "face" or "side", is used as the simplified character for 麵 ,（miàn, ㄇㄧㄢˋ）"noodle". This raises the question: does the sentence " 她在下面 "（tā zài xià miàn, ㄊㄚ ㄗㄞˋ ㄒㄧㄚˋ ㄇㄧㄢˋ）mean "She is cooking noodles" or "She is in a lower position"?

Similarly, treating 后 as the simplified character for 後 creates ambiguity in the phrase 皇后有幾個隨從（huáng hǒu yǒu jǐ gè suí cóng, ㄏㄨㄤˊㄏㄡˋ ㄧㄡˇ ㄐㄧˇ ㄍㄜˋ ㄙㄨㄟˊ ㄘㄨㄥˊ）: does it mean "There are several attendants behind the emperor" or "The empress has several attendants"?

125

漢字之所以成為中國統一的基本，原因之一是大家都可以用任何方言來讀漢字。但是在設計簡化字的時候，沒有考慮

到漢字的各種方言讀音。例如，閩南語的「面」bīn 和「麵」mī，「后」hiō 和「後」āu，它們即不是同音字也不是同義字，把「面」和「后」來分別當作「麵」和「後」的簡化字出現字義混亂並不出奇。簡體字就不存在這些問題，例如，閩南語的「云」和「雲」都讀 hun，「气」和「氣」都讀 khi。

One reason why Chinese characters serve as a unifying foundation for China is that they can be pronounced in any dialect. However, when designing simplified characters, the various dialectal pronunciations of Chinese characters were not taken into account. For example, in Hokkien, 面（bīn）and 麵（mī）are not homophones, nor are 后（hiō）and 後（āu）. It is not surprising that treating 面 and 后 as simplified forms of 麵 and 後 leads to confusion in meaning. In contrast, simple characters do not have these issues; for instance, both 云 and 雲 are pronounced as "hun", and both 气 and 氣 are pronounced as "khi" in Hokkien.

126

簡化字並非一無是處。

我們將「郁闷」和「鬱悶」比較。「郁」是「鬱」的簡化字；「闷」是「悶」的簡體字。「郁」的字義是「富有的城域」；「鬱」的字義是「樹木叢林」。「郁」和「鬱」是同音字，都讀 yù（ㄩˋ）。「鬱」被當作假借字用在「鬱悶」，我們何不把「郁」也當作假借字，取代「鬱」呢？您不覺得「郁」比「鬱」易認易寫嗎？

Simplified characters are not all entirely without merit.

Let’s compare 郁 （yù mèn, ㄩˋㄇㄣˋ）and 鬱悶（yù mèn, ㄩˋㄇㄣˋ）. They are the same words meaning “melancholy”. 郁」is the simplified character of 鬱 , while is the simple form of 悶 . The original meaning of 郁 is “a prosperous place”, and 鬱 means “dense woods”. Since 郁 and 鬱 are homophones sharing the same pronunciation yù（ㄩˋ）, both can be used as phonetic loan characters in the word 鬱悶 . Why not use 郁 as a substitute loan character instead? Don’t you think 郁 is easier to recognize and write than 鬱 ?

127

漢字的形成是約定俗成，甚至有些字來自積非成是，簡化字也不外如此。中國官方法定的簡化字已經廣泛使用，自成一體，並且從總體來講，大多數的簡化字實際上是簡體字，能引起字義不清的簡化字為數極少。人們同時使用繁體字和簡化字已經是不可改變的事實。我們應該避免使用字義混淆的簡化字，比如，不要將「麵店」寫成「面店」。也許台灣朋友會以為「面店」是「美容店」。

The formation of Chinese characters has been shaped by convention. Some characters even gained acceptance despite originally being erroneous, and simplified characters are no exception. The official simplified characters defined by the Chinese government are now widely used and form a cohesive system. Overall, most simplified characters are just simple characters, with very few causing ambiguities in meaning. The simultaneous use of traditional and simplified characters is an established fact that cannot be changed. However, we should avoid using simplified characters that may cause confusion, such as refraining from writing 店（miàn diàn, ㄇㄧㄢˋ ㄉㄧㄢˋ）, noodle shop, as 面店（miàn diàn, ㄇㄧㄢˋ ㄉㄧㄢˋ）, "face shop". Taiwanese friends might think that 面店 refers to a "beauty salon".

128

漢字除了有簡體字、繁體字、簡化字之分，還有一些漢字有異體字之別，例如，「回、囬、囘」、「麵、麪」、「夠、够」、「豬、猪」等等。

In addition to simple, complex and simplified characters, some Chinese characters have variant forms called 異體字（yì tǐ zì, ㄧˋㄊㄧˇㄗˋ）, "he variant form of a character". For example, 回、囬、囘（huí, ㄏㄨㄟˊ）"back", and 麪（miàn, ㄇㄧㄢˋ）"noodle", 夠 and 够（gòu, ㄍㄡˋ）"enough", and 豬 and 猪（zhū ㄓㄨ）"pig".

十九 漢字拉丁化的失敗

The Failure of Chinese Character Latinization

129

強盛的清帝國在十九世紀末二十世紀初走向沒落，世界列強瓜分中國，大多數的知識分子尋找不到民族垂危的原因，他們甚至歸罪於中國數千年的漢字已經不合時宜，主張漢字拉丁化，當時文豪魯迅更是絕望地高喊「漢字不滅，中國必亡」。漢字拉丁化似乎成為必然之勢。

By the late 19th and early 20th centuries, the once-powerful Qing Dynasty was in decline, and foreign powers were carving up Chinese territory. Chinese intellectuals, deeply troubled by the nation's crisis, began questioning how a once-strong nation had fallen so far. Some attributed the nation's troubles to the centuries-old Chinese writing system, declaring it outdated and calling for its abandonment in favor of Latinization. Lu Xun, the renowned literary master, despairingly declared, "If Chinese characters are not destroyed, then China will die. " At that time, the Latinization of Chinese characters seemed inevitable.

130

在二十世紀五十年代，中國大陸試行漢字拉丁化，即是用拼音拉丁字母代替漢字，但是最終行不通，原因是漢字是表意符號，跨越方言，克服方言的差別，可以用任何方言來讀。拼音只是普通話讀音。普通話是一種北方方言，即使是普通話讀出來的同音字也很多，比如「籮、鑼、蘿、騾、裸」都是 luó，又如同音詞語「公雞、攻擊、功績」都是 gōng jī，拉丁化會引起混亂。

In the 1950s, mainland China experimented with the Latinization of Chinese characters, replacing them with Latin alphabet-based pinyin. However, this approach ultimately proved unfeasible because Chinese characters are logographic symbols, allowing people to read across dialects and overcome regional differences. Pinyin, on the other hand, only represents Putonghua pronunciation, which is a northern dialect. Even within Putonghua, there are many homophones; for instance, 籮 “basket”, 鑼 “gong”, 蘿 “radish”, 騾 “mule”, and 裸 “naked”are all pronounced luó. Similarly, homophones like 公雞 , “rooster, 攻擊 , “attack, and 功績 , “achievement”, are all pronounced gōng jī. Thus, Romanization would introduce significant confusion.

131

兩千多年前，秦始皇統一文字，只是統一書體，沒有統一字音。

方言是無法消滅的，假如漢字消滅，表音的拼音字母很容易結合地區方言變成全新的文字。新文字會助長地方政治體的出現，國家容易出現分裂局面，中國統一不堪矣！

More than two thousand years ago, Emperor Qin Shi Huang unified the writing system of Chinese characters, but did not standardize the pronunciations.

It is impossible to eliminate dialects. If Chinese characters are abolished, phonetic alphabets could easily merge with regional dialects to form entirely new scripts. Such new scripts could encourage the rise of local political entities, making national fragmentation more likely and threatening China's unity.

132

今天，漢字沒有滅。中國也沒有亡。相反地，中國的復興使許多國家掀起了學習漢字的熱潮。

Today, Chinese characters are not eliminated, and China is standing tall. On the contrary, China's resurgence has sparked a wave of interest in learning Chinese characters in many countries.

二十 漢字的注音

Phonetic Notations of Chinese Characters

133

每一個漢字都是單音字。近代為了翻譯外國量詞，創造了個別的漢字是讀兩個字音的，它們不是雙音節，因為字音和音節是不同的。字音含有意思，音節只是發音。例如：浬 讀兩個字音「海里」，瓩 讀「千瓦」，「吋」讀「英寸」。

Every Chinese character is monosyllabic. In modern times, some individual Chinese characters were created to translate the foreign units of measurements. These characters are pronounced with two syllables and combine two meanings. For example, 浬 reads 海里（hǎi lǐ, ㄏㄞˇㄌㄧˇ）"nautical mile", 瓩 reads 千瓦（qiān wǎ, ㄑㄧㄚˇ）"kilowatt", and 吋 reads 英寸（yīng cùn, ㄧㄥ ㄘㄨㄣˋ）"British inch".

漢字的讀音由聲母音、韻母音和聲調構成，例如，媽（mā, ㄇㄚ ）、麻（má, ㄇㄚˊ）、馬（mǎ, ㄇㄚˇ）、罵（mà, ㄇㄚˋ）。拼音字母 m 和注音符號ㄇ是聲母音符號，拼音字母 a 和注音符號ㄚ是韻母音符號，「陰 ˉ 、陽 ˊ 、上 ˇ 、去 ˋ 」為國語的四聲調符號。漢語的字音不一定含有聲母音，但是必須有韻母音和聲調，例如，挨（āi，ㄞ）、捱（ái, ㄞˊ）、矮（ǎi, ㄠˇ）、愛（ài, ㄞˋ），等等。

The pronunciation of a Chinese character usually consists of a consonant, a vowel and tone. For example, the characters 媽（mā, ㄇㄚ）“mother”, 麻（má, ㄇㄚˊ）“hemp”, 馬（mǎ, ㄇㄚˇ）“horse”, 罵（mà, ㄇㄚˋ）, “scold”, illustrate this structure.

The Pinyin letter “m” and the Mandarin Phonetic Symbol “ㄇ” represent the consonant（聲母）.

The Pinyin letter “a” and the Mandarin Phonetic Symbol “ㄚ” represent the vowel（韻母）.

The tone marks “-”（first tone, the high-and-level tone）, “ˊ”（second tone, the rising tone）, “ˇ”（third tone, the falling-and-rising tone）, and “ˋ”（fourth tone, the falling tone）denote the four tones of Mandarin.

In Mandarin, the pronunciation of a Chinese character does not necessarily include a consonant, but it must contain a vowel and tone. For example, 挨（āi，ㄞ）“lean on”, 捱（ái, ㄞˊ）“suffer”, 矮（ǎi, ㄠˇ）“short”, and 愛（ài，ㄞˋ）“love”, have no consonant.

134

口頭教授法

（kǒu tóu jiāo shòu fǎ, ㄎㄡˇ ㄊㄡˊ ㄐㄧㄠ ㄕㄡˋ ㄈㄚˇ）

The Oral Teaching Method

漢字是表意文字，不是表音文字，所以，初始漢字沒有注音，每個字的讀音都要靠口頭教授。即使是今天，許多人識字還是靠這個古老的方法。

Chinese characters are logographic, meaning they represent ideas or concepts rather than sounds, so early Chinese characters did not have phonetic notation. Each character's pronunciation had to be taught orally. Even today, many people learn to read and write through this ancient method of oral instruction.

在《康熙字典》裡，如此講述了口頭教學文字的情況，「證鄉談法：鄉談豈但分南北，每郡相鄰便不同。由此故教音韻證，不因指示甚難明。」

In the "Kang Xi Dictionary", the oral instruction of pronunciations of Chinese characters is described as follows, "In the local dialects, the way of speaking is not just divided by north and south; even neighboring counties can differ. Therefore, phonetics and rhymes become very difficult to clarify without direct demonstration."

This highlights the challenges of teaching pronunciation in Chinese due to variations in dialects, which complicate the process of conveying the correct sounds through written characters alone.

135

漢字在積累越來越多的過程中，先後出現了直音法、反

切、威妥瑪氏拼音法、國語注音符號和中文拼音字母（應該準確的說，是普通話拼音字母）等幾種注音法。這些注音法是一脈相承的。

With the accumulation of Chinese characters over time, several phonetic notation systems emerged, including the 直音法（zhí yīn fǎ）, 反切（fǎn qiè）, Wade-Giles system, Mandarin Phonetic Symbols（Bopomofo）, and Pinyin（more accurately referred to as“Putonghua Pinyin”）. These phonetic systems are all interconnected.

136

直音法

直音法也叫「讀若某」，即是用同音字注音，是最早的注音法，例如，「陽，讀若羊」，「陽」與「羊」是同音字。由於幾乎每個字都有多個同音字，所以用同音字來注音，就大量地減少了口頭教學的工作量，但是前提必須是先要學懂一些字的讀音，在這個例子中，如果你不懂讀「羊」字，就無法讀「陽」字。至今許多人還使用「讀若某」的方法來學習和記憶漢字讀音。

直音法（zhí yīn fǎ）, the Direct Phonetic Method, is also known as 讀若某 “Dú ruò mǒu”. It involves using homophones to indicate pronunciation and is one of the earliest phonetic notation systems. For example, one would say " 陽 reads as 羊 ". The pronunciation of the character 陽（yáng, 一尢ˊ）"sun", is indicated by the homophone 羊（yáng, 一尢ˊ）"sheep".

Since most Chinese characters have multiple homophones, this method significantly reduces the workload of oral teaching. However, the prerequisite is that one must first understand the pronunciation of certain characters. In this example, if you do not know how to read the character 羊 , you will be unable to read 陽 . Today, many people still use this method to learn and memorize the pronunciations of Chinese characters.

137

反切注音法

反切注音法創制於東漢年代（西元 25-220 年）。它是以一個字的聲母音和另一個字的韻母音互相切入而成的一個讀音。例如，「陽，移章切」，「移」的聲母音，「章」的韻母音。在這個例子中，如果不懂得讀「移」和「章」，就無法讀「陽」。

反切注音法第一次將字音分解成聲母音和韻母音，是漢語語音學的一個飛躍發展。

古代字典都使用反切注音法。

反切注音法 , "Fanqie Phonetic Notation Method", was developed during the Eastern Han Dynasty（25-220 AD）. It involves using the initial consonant of one character and the final vowel of another character to create a pronunciation.

For example, one would say " 陽，移章切 ". 陽（yáng, ㄧㄤˊ）, "sun", is pronounced using 移（yí, ㄧˊ）, "move", for its initial consonant and 章（zhāng, ㄓㄤ）, "article", for its final vowel. If one does not know how to read 移 and 章 , they would not be able to pronounce 陽 .

The Fanqie method was the first to decompose a character's pronunciation into its initial consonant and final vowel, representing a significant advancement in Chinese phonetics. The Fanqie phonetic notation system was commonly used in ancient dictionaries.

138

威妥瑪氏拼音（Wade-Giles System）和郵政拼音（Postal Romanization）

威妥瑪氏拼音（Wade-Giles System）簡稱威氏拼音，是一套用於拼寫中文國語讀音的羅馬字母拼音系統。它是在十九世紀中葉，由英國人威妥瑪 Thomas Francis Wade 創造，後來翟理斯 H.A. Giles 加以修改完善，合稱 Wade-Giles System。郵政拼音（Postal Romanization）是一套用於拼寫中國人名和地名的羅馬字母拼音系統，1906 年春季於上海舉行的帝國郵電聯席會議通過其使用。威氏拼音和郵政拼音一直使用至 1958 年中國大陸推廣中文拼音後，才逐步廢止。

郵政拼音拼寫的地區方言地名到 20 世紀 80 年代，才改用中文拼音，例如，郵政拼音 Peking（北京）改用中文拼音 Beijing，Canton（廣東）改為 Guang Dong,，以及 Amoy（廈門）改為 Xia Men。

一些威氏拼音和郵政拼音的地名、專用名詞、人名還繼續使用，例如，Tibet（西藏）、Mongolia（蒙古）、Tai Chi（太極）、Kungfu（功夫）、Sun Yat-sen（孫逸仙），等等。

台灣和香港地區仍然使用威氏拼音和郵政拼音，例如，Hong Kong（香港）、Kowloon（九龍）、Taipei（台北）、Kaohsiung（高雄），等等。

The Wade-Giles System and the Postal Romanization

The Wade-Giles system is a Romanization system used to spell the pronunciation of Mandarin. It was created in the mid-19th century by the British scholar Thomas Francis Wade and later revised by H.A. Giles, hence the name Wade-Giles system.

The Postal Romanization is another system for spelling Chinese names and places using Roman letters, which was adopted during the Imperial Postal Conference held in Shanghai in the spring of 1906. Both the Wade-Giles system and Postal Romanization continued to be used until 1958 when Pinyin was promoted in mainland China, leading to their gradual obsolescence.

The Romanization of names of places in regional dialects using Postal Romanization was not replaced with Pinyin until the 1980s. For example, the Postal Romanization "Peking"（北京）was changed to “Beijing”, “Canton”（廣東）was changed to “Guangdong”, and “Amoy”（廈門）was changed to “Xiamen”.

The names of some places, proper nouns, and personal names from the Wade-Giles and Postal Romanization systems continue to be used, such as Tibet（西藏）, Mongolia（蒙古）, Taichi（太極）. Kungfu（功夫）and Sun Yat-sen（孫逸仙）, among others.

Taiwan and Hong Kong still use the Wade-Giles and Postal Romanization systems. For example, Hong Kong（香港）, Kowloon（九龍）, Taipei（台北）, and Kaohsiung（高雄）, among others.

威妥瑪 Thomas Francis Wade 十分精通反切注音法，他用羅馬的輔音字母來代替漢字的聲母音，用羅馬的元音字母來代替漢字的韻母音，發明了威氏拼音法。例如，yang（陽），輔音字母 y 代替「移」的聲母音，元音字母 ang 代替「章」的韻母音，「陽，移章切」變成「陽 yang」的羅馬拼音。

Thomas Francis Wade was highly proficient in the Fanqie phonetic notation method. He replaced the initial consonants of Chinese characters with Roman consonant letters and the final vowels with Roman vowel letters, inventing the Wade phonetic system. For example, in the case of 陽（yáng, ㄧㄤˊ）, the consonant letter “y” replaces the initial sound of 移（yí, ㄧˊ）, while the vowel letters “ang” replace the final sound of 章（zhāng, ㄓㄤ）. Thus, 陽，移章切 becomes the Romanized spelling “yang”.

威氏拼音（Wade-Giles system）的羅馬字母

The Wade-Giles Transcription System

聲母 Consonants：p[b] p`[p] m[m] f[f], t[d] t`[t] n[n] l[l], k[g] k`[k] h[h], ch[j] ch`[q] hs[x], ch[zh] ch`[ch] sh[sh], j[r] 日, ts[z] ts`[c] s[s].

單韻母 Single vowels: a e i o u

139

國語注音符號

國語注音符號是標準國語標音系統之一，1912 年制定，1918 年開始使用。至今，國語注音符號一直是漢字的主要拼讀工具之一。

The Mandarin Phonetic Symbols is one of the standard Mandarin phonetic systems. It is created in 1912 and started using in 1918. The Mandarin Phonetic Symbols has become a main method of Mandarin phonetic until now.

Mandarin Phonetic Symbols, one of the standard phonetic systems for Mandarin, was established in 1912 and came into use in 1918. To this day, Mandarin Phonetic Symbols remain one of the primary tools for phonetic reading of Chinese characters.

國語注音符號是由一批留日的中國學者創造的。他們模仿日文假名，簡化古漢字偏旁，創造了注音符號。他們利用注音符號取代威氏拼音 Wade-Giles System 的羅馬字母，對每一個國語注音符號都用漢字標明讀音，同時加入國語四聲符號，使其拼音聲調準確，例如，採用國語注音符號「陽ㄧㄤˊ」取代威氏拼音「陽 yang」。

The Mandarin Phonetic Symbols was created by a group of Chinese scholars who had studied in Japan. They modeled the symbols after Japanese kana and simplified ancient Chinese character components to create Mandarin phonetic symbols. These symbols were used to replace the Roman letters of the Wade-Giles System, with each symbol indicating pronunciation using Chinese characters, and added the four tones of Mandarin to ensure accurate Mandarin intonations. For example, for the character 陽 , "sun", the Mandarin Phonetic Symbol "ㄧㄤˊ" was used to replace the Wade-Giles System "yang".

國語注音符號

The Mandarin Phonetic Symbols

聲母 Consonants	介母 Head vowels	韻母 Vowels
ㄅ坡 ㄆ破 ㄇ摸 ㄈ佛 ㄉ得 ㄊ特 ㄋ訥 ㄌ勒 ㄍ哥 ㄎ科 ㄏ喝 ㄐ基 ㄑ欺 ㄒ希 ㄓ知 ㄔ蚩 ㄕ詩 ㄖ日 ㄗ資 ㄘ雌 ㄙ思	ㄧ衣 ㄨ烏 ㄩ迂	ㄚ啊 ㄛ喔 ㄝ鵝 ㄞ哀 ㄟ欸 ㄠ熬 ㄡ歐 ㄢ安 ㄣ恩 ㄤ昂 ㄥ 哼的韻母 ㄦ 兒

四聲

The four tones of Mandarin intonation

陰平 high-and-level tone	陽平 rising tone	上聲 falling-and-rising tone	去聲 falling tone
ˉ	ˊ	ˇ	ˋ
媽 ㄇㄚ mother	麻 ㄇㄚˊ hemp	馬 ㄇㄚˇ horse	罵 ㄇㄚˋ scold

「莊」(ㄓㄨㄤ) 字的注音包括了聲母ㄓ、介母ㄨ、韻母ㄤ。

The consonant ㄓ, head vowel ㄨand vowel ㄤ are all found in the character 莊（ㄓㄨㄤ）, “village”.

140

中文拼音字母

1955 至 1957 年中國文字改革委員會制定《中文拼音方案》，作為一種漢字拼音方法。1958 年 2 月 11 日全國人民代表大會批准公佈《中文拼音方案》。從此，拼音字母逐步取代威妥瑪氏拼音字母。

Pinyin Alphabet

From 1955 to 1957, the Chinese Language Reform Committee created the Pinyin Scheme as a method for phoneticizing Chinese characters. On February 11, 1958, the National People's Congress officially approved and announced the scheme. From then on, Pinyin letters gradually replaced the Wade-Giles romanization system.

141

中文拼音方案

The Pinyin Scheme

(1) 字母表 The Pinyin Alphabet

字母 The Pinyin letters: Aa Bb Cc Dd Ee Ff Gg

ㄚ ㄅㄝ ㄘㄝ ㄉㄝ ㄜ ㄝㄈ ㄍㄝ

Hh	Ii	Jj	Kk	Ll	Mm	Nn
ㄏㄚ	ㄧ	ㄐㄧㄝ	ㄎㄝ	ㄝㄌ	ㄝㄇ	ㄋㄝ
Oo	Pp	Qq	Rr	Ss	Tt	
ㄛ	ㄆㄝ	ㄑㄧㄡ	ㄚㄦ	ㄝㄙ	ㄊㄝ	
Uu	Vv	Ww	Xx	Yy	Zz	
ㄨ	ㄪㄝ	ㄨㄚ	ㄒㄧ	ㄧㄚ	ㄗㄝ	

(2) 聲母表 **The Consonants**

b	p	m	f	d	t	n	l
ㄅ玻	ㄆ坡	ㄇ摸	ㄈ佛	ㄉ得	ㄊ特	ㄋ訥	ㄌ勒
g	k	h			j	q	x
ㄍ哥	ㄎ科	ㄏ喝			ㄐ基	ㄑ欺	ㄒ希
zh	ch	sh	r		z	c	s
ㄓ知	ㄔ蚩	ㄕ詩	ㄖ日		ㄗ資	ㄘ雌	ㄙ思

(3) 韻母表 The Vowels

i ㄧ 衣	u ㄨ 烏	ǖ ㄩ 迂
a ㄚ 啊	ia ㄧㄚ 呀	ua ㄨㄚ 蛙
uo ㄛ 喔		ㄛ 窩
e ㄜ 鵝	ie ㄧㄝ 耶	ǖe ㄨㄝ 約
ai ㄞ 哀		uai ㄨㄞ 歪

ei ㄟ 欸	uei ㄨㄟ 威		
ao ㄠ 熬	iao ㄧㄠ 腰		
ou ㄡ 歐	iou ㄧㄡ 憂		
an ㄢ 安	ian ㄧㄢ 煙	uan ㄢ 彎	üan ㄩㄢ 冤
en ㄣ 恩	in ㄧㄣ 因	uen ㄨㄣ 溫	ün ㄩㄣ 暈
ang ㄤ 昂	iang ㄧㄤ 央	uang ㄨㄤ 汪	
eng ㄥ 亨的韻母	ing ㄧㄥ 英	ueng ㄨㄥ 翁	
ong ㄨㄥ 轟的韻母	iong ㄩㄥ 雍		

(4) 聲調符號
The four tones

ˉ	ˊ	ˇ	ˋ
陰平 high-and-level tone	陽平 rising tone	上聲 falling-and-rising tone	去聲 falling tone

《中文拼音方案》全盤採用國語注音符號的方法，只不過用英語字母代替國語注音符號，是為了漢字拉丁化做準備，可

是漢字拉丁化不成功。中文拼音也錯有錯著，成為普通話音標和拉丁字母文字轉寫中國人名和地名。而且，為拉丁字母文字的使用者更加容易接受。這也是為什麼既有國語注音符號又有拼音字母兩套注音工具。

The Pinyin Scheme fully adopted the approach of the Mandarin Phonetic Symbols, simply replacing the symbols with Latin letters. This was initially intended as a step toward the Latinization of Chinese characters; however, this Latinization effort was not successful. Despite this, Pinyin has taken on a new role, becoming both a phonetic notation system for Mandarin and a method for transcribing Chinese names and places into Latin spelling. This system is more accessible for users of the Latin alphabet, which is why both Mandarin Phonetic Symbols and Pinyin exist as phonetic tools for Chinese characters.

許多書的文字是由右向左縱向排列的。在這些書的字裡行間加注國語注音符號是容易寫上的，但是要加注拼音字母就很難。這是因為拼音字母原本不是作為注音工具，而是為了漢字拉丁化做準備的。

In many books, the Chinese characters are arranged vertically from right to left. It is relatively easy to add Mandarin Phonetic Symbols between the lines in these books, but adding Pinyin is much more difficult. This is because Pinyin was not originally designed as a phonetic annotation tool but was instead intended as a step toward the Latinization of Chinese characters.

人（ㄖㄣˊ）之（ㄓ）初（ㄔㄨ），

性（ㄒㄧㄥˋ）本（ㄅㄣˇ）善（ㄕㄢˋ）。

142

從 1979 年 6 月 15 日起，聯合國秘書處採用中文拼音字母作為在各種拉丁字母文字中轉寫中華人民共和國人名地名的標準，取代了威氏拼音和郵政拼音法。

Since June 15, 1979, the United Nations Secretariat has used Pinyin as the standard for transcribing names and places of the People's Republic of China into Latin spelling, replacing the Wade-Giles and Postal Romanization systems.

143

自 1982 年中文拼音國際化後，中國大陸的漢語專用名詞、地名、人名，它們的拉丁文翻譯，使用中文拼音字母。

Since the internationalization of Pinyin in 1982, the Latin transliterations of Chinese-specific terms, places, and personal names in mainland China have used Pinyin.

144

威妥瑪氏音標、國語注音符號、中文拼音字母的比較

Comparation of the Wade-Gile System, Mandarin Phonetic Symbols and Hanyu Pinyin Alphabet

年代 Age	注音法 Method	字母比較 Comparison of Alphabets and Symbols
十九世紀中葉 Mid-19th century	威妥瑪氏音標 Wade-Giles System	聲母 Consonants p[b] p`[p] m[m] f[f] t[d] t`[t] n[n] l[l] k[g] k`[k] h[h] ch[j] ch`[q] hs[x] ch[zh] ch`[ch] sh[sh] j[r] ts[z] ts`[c] s[s] 單韻母 Singal vowels a e i o u
1918	國語注音符號 Mandarin Phonetic Symbols	聲母 Consonants ㄅ玻 ㄆ坡 ㄇ摸 ㄈ佛 ㄉ得 ㄊ特 ㄋ訥 ㄌ勒 ㄍ哥 ㄎ科 ㄏ喝 ㄐ基 ㄑ欺 ㄒ希 ㄓ知 ㄔ蚩 ㄕ詩 ㄖ日 ㄗ資 ㄘ雌 ㄙ思 介母 Head vowels ㄧ衣 ㄨ烏 ㄩ迂 單韻母 Singal vowels ㄚ阿 ㄛ哦 ㄜ鵝 ㄧ衣 ㄨ烏 ㄩ迂 ㄝ (耶的韻母聲)

1958	中文拼音字母 Hanyu Pinyin Alphabet (the Scheme for the Chinese Phonetic Alphabet)	聲母 Consonants b 玻 p 坡 m 摸 f 佛 d 得 t 特 n 訥 l 勒 g 哥 k 科 h 喝 j 基 q 欺 x 希 zh 知 ch 蚩 sh 詩 r 日 z 資 c 雌 s 思 單韻母 Single vowels a 阿 o 哦 e 鵝 i 衣 u 烏 ü 迂

三種注音方法的先後出現時序是威妥瑪氏音標、國語注音符號、中文拼音字母，它們是一脈相承的。

The sequence of appearance for these three phonetic systems is: Wade-Giles System, Mandarin Phonetic Symbols, and Pinyin. They are inherited through a continuous line.

145

經過對照比較，容易看出威妥瑪氏音標為其後的國語注音符號提供了參考，更被後來的中文拼音字母所複製。

Through comparison, it is easy to see that the Wade-Giles System provided a reference for the later Mandarin Phonetic Symbols, which was further adapted by the subsequent Pinyin system.

真想不到，英國人威妥瑪 Thomas Francis Wade 和翟理斯 H.A. Giles 竟然是國語注音符號和中文拼音字母的鼻祖。

It's hard to believe that the British, Thomas Francis Wade and H.A. Giles, are actually the pioneers of Mandarin Phonetic Symbols and Pinyin.

二十一 甲骨文之謎

The Mystery of Oracle Bone Scripts

146

（摘自《漢字的文化史》，藤枝晃・日本）

甲骨文的發現是戲劇般的偶然的。

The discovery of Oracle Bone scripts was dramatic and fortuitous.

147

晚清時期（十九世紀末、二十世紀初）在河南安陽縣，農民挖地時常常挖到一些有刻紋的龜甲和牛肩胛骨，他們稱之為「龍骨」，以賤價賣給藥材鋪。

During the late Qing Dynasty（the late 19th and early 20th centuries）in Anyang County, Henan, farmers often unearthed tortoise shells and cow shoulder bones with inscriptions while digging. They referred to these as “dragon bones” and sold them at low prices to Chinese herb shops.

148

清朝光緒年間（19 世紀末）國子監王懿榮（1845—1900）偶然在中藥材中發現「龍骨」上的文字，立即派人收集，開展整理及研究工作，使埋藏地下數千年的甲骨文重見天日。

During the Guangxu era of the Qing Dynasty（late 19th century）, Wang Yi Rong（1845–1900）, the head scholar of the

Imperial Academy, accidentally discovered inscriptions on the "dragon bones" among Chinese herbs. He promptly sent people to collect, organize, and study them, bringing back to light the oracle bone scripts that had been buried for thousands of years.

149

商朝的甲骨文經過三千多年到了清朝末年才偶然被發現，而在這幾千年的史料記載中無一言半語與甲骨文有關，甚至民間傳説都沒有。甲骨文在這幾千年中銷聲匿跡而不留半點蛛絲馬跡，這是為什麼？到目前為止，尚是一個不解之謎。

The oracle bone scripts from the Shang Dynasty went undiscovered for over three thousand years until it was accidentally found in the late Qing Dynasty. Throughout these thousands of years, there were no historical records mentioning the oracle bone scripts, not even in folklore. These scripts remained unknown and left no trace during this long period. It is now still an unsolved mystery.

二十二 漢字原先是溝通神靈的文字

Chinese Characters were originally Symbols used for Communicating with the Deities

150

甲骨文是最古老的漢字，人們用來與神靈對話，而不是用於人們之間的文字交流。

The Oracle bone script is the oldest form of Chinese characters, used by people to communicate with deities rather than for written communication among themselves.

151

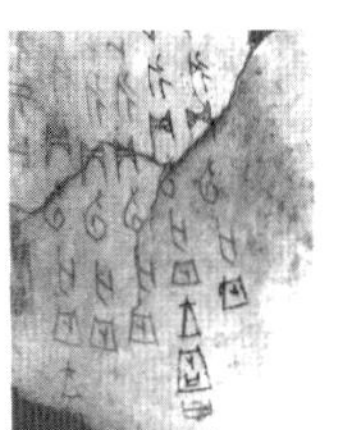

占卜一例 **a divination**

（京都大學人文科學研究所藏）

摘自《漢字的文化史》

漢字原先用來與神靈對話，甲骨文是用來占卜的。

上圖甲骨文的第一行是「癸丑卜、永貞、旬亡禍？」，意思是：「在癸丑這一天占卜，有一位名叫『永』的貞人卜問，從今天起的十天內，我王有沒有禍事呢？」(引自日本的漢字學家藤枝晃的《漢字的文化史》)。貞人根據燒灼甲骨出現的爆裂，辨別神的答覆。

Chinese characters were originally used for communicating with deities, and the oracle bone script was specifically used for divination.

The first line on the above oracle bone script reads: " 癸丑卜、永貞、旬亡禍？" This translates to: "On the day of Gui Chou, a diviner named 'Yong' asked, 'Will there be any calamities for our king within the next ten days?'" (Quoted from the Japanese sinologist Akira Fujieda's The Cultural History of Chinese Characters) . The diviner would then interpret the cracks that appeared on the burned oracle bones to discern the response from the deities.

152

測字（cè zì, ㄘㄜˋ ㄗˋ）"Ce Zi"

Divination through Chinese Characters

測字應該是由甲骨文占卜衍生的。有人相信漢字含有暗示密碼，於是有算命先生利用測字，替人預測吉凶，教人趨吉避凶。

測字（cè zì, ㄘㄜˋ ㄗˋ）"Ce Zi", the divination through Chinese characters, is believed to be derived from the divination practices of the Oracle Bone script. Some people believe that Chinese characters contain hidden codes, which has led fortune tellers to use character divination to predict fortunes for others, enabling them to seek good luck and avoid misfortune.

153

漢字能給人們帶來好運。

Many people believe that Chinese characters can bring good luck.

福祿壽三星

The Three Star Gods of 福星（fú xīng, ㄈㄨˊ ㄒㄧㄥ）"Fu Xing", the God of Fortune, 祿星（lù xīng, ㄌㄨˋㄒㄧㄥ）"Lu Xing", the God of Emolument, and 壽星（shóu xīng, ㄕㄡˋ ㄊㄨˊ）

"Shou Xing", the God of Longevity.

中國民眾普遍喜好福祿壽三星。

The Chinese people have a fondness for the Three Star Gods of Fortune, Emolument, and Longevity. These three deities are often depicted together in Chinese culture and are associated with bringing good luck, wealth, and health.

百福圖（bǎi Fú tú, ㄅㄞˇ ㄈㄨˊ ㄊㄨˊ）

The Calligraphy of Hundred 福

百福圖有「福」字的一百種寫法。

The Calligraphy of Hundred 福 features one hundred different ways of writing the character 福（fú, ㄈㄨˊ）, which means "blessing" or "good fortune.

百祿圖（bǎi lù tú, ㄅㄞˇ ㄌㄨˋ ㄊㄨˊ）

The Calligraphy of Hundred 祿

百祿圖是「祿」字的一百種寫法。

The Calligraphy of Hundred 祿 features one hundred different ways of writing the character 祿（lù, ㄌㄨˋ）, which means “emolument”.

百壽圖（bǎi shòu tú, ㄅㄞˇ ㄕㄡˋ ㄊㄨˊ）

The Calligraphy of Hundred 壽

百壽圖有一百種「壽」字的寫法。

The Calligraphy of Hundred 壽 features one hundred different ways of writing the character " 壽 "（shòu, ㄕㄡˋ）, which means "longevity".

154

囍 (shuāng xǐ, ㄕㄨㄤ ㄒㄧˇ)

Double joy

婚宴必有的裝飾。

The decorative red banner with the character 囍 is essential for a Chinese wedding banquet.

「喜」字甲骨文, = 打鼓慶祝 + 笑得合不攏嘴。祝福一對新人 囍。

喜 (xǐ, ㄒㄧˇ) "joy". Its oracle bone script consists of , "drumming", and , "grinning from ear to ear". We wish the bride and bridegroom 囍 (shuāng xǐ, ㄕㄨㄤ ㄒㄧˇ), "double joy".

155

「恭喜發財」是農曆年最常見的賀年揮春和祝福。

恭喜發財（gōng xǐ fā cái, ㄍㄨㄥ ㄒㄧˇ ㄈㄚ ㄘㄞˊ）is the most common New Year greeting and blessing during the Lunar New Year.

This phrase translates to "Wishing you prosperity", and is often used to convey good wishes for wealth and success in the coming year. It's a traditional phrase frequently seen on decorative couplets and banners during the festivities.

156

「豬頭肥」病患者

A mumps patient

信不信由你，漢字可以治病，儘管毫無科學根據。腮腺炎俗稱「豬頭肥」，民間有人在「豬頭肥」患處寫上「虎」字，「畫虎吃豬」作為治療腮腺炎的方法。

Believe it or not, Chinese characters have healing abilities, even though there is no scientific basis for it. Mumps is commonly referred to as 豬頭肥（zhū tóu féi, ㄓㄨ ㄊㄡˊㄈㄟˊ）"pig head fat", due to the swelling that occurs on the sides of the face. In folk tradition, some people write the character 虎（hǔ, ㄏㄨˇ）"tiger", on the swollen area, depicting a tiger eating a pig as a remedy for mumps.

二十三　書法

Chinese Calligraphy

157

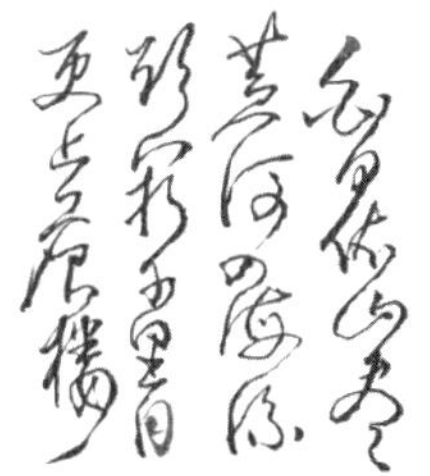

狂草書法

Highly cursive script of Chinese calligraphy

唐詩《登鸛雀樓》：白日依山盡，黃河入海流。欲窮千里目，更上一層樓。

Quotation from the Tang poem "On Guan Que Lou Tower":

The white sun sets behind the mountains,

The Yellow River flows into the sea.

To broaden one's view of a thousand miles,

One must ascend another floor.

為什麼漢字文化與書法藝術有著深刻而內在的聯繫？因為

漢字是由象形演變而成，所以可以昇華為一種視覺藝術。書法是中國文化的國粹，堪比中國功夫、戲劇，甚至有些書法價值連城。

Why is there a profound and intrinsic connection between the culture of Chinese characters and the art of calligraphy? This is because Chinese characters evolved from pictographs, allowing them to transform into a form of visual art. Calligraphy is a national treasure of Chinese culture, comparable to Chinese martial arts and traditional theater, with some calligraphic works considered priceless masterpieces.

如何欣賞書法，見仁見智，但是只有中國文化修養的人，才懂得欣賞。一些外國朋友通過練習書法，提高自己的文化修養。

Appreciating calligraphy is subjective; each person sees it differently. However, only those with a grounding in Chinese culture truly understand its beauty. Some foreigners also practice Chinese calligraphy to deepen their cultural appreciation and understanding.

二十四　古老的中國的符號文化

The Ancient Chinese Semiotics

158

中國古人創造的符號文化，不僅有文字符號，還有八卦符號和符籙符號。文字是明顯意義的符號，而八卦和符籙是隱含義和迷思的符號。因為八卦和符籙是迷思的，神秘莫測，所以不如文字那麼廣泛使用。

The semiotics created by ancient Chinese people include not only Chinese characters but also Ba Gua（The Eight Diagrams）symbols and Fu Lu talisman symbols（The Taoist Magic Figures）. Written Chinese characters are symbols with clear meanings, while the Ba Gua and Fu Lu talismans are symbols with hidden meanings and mystical elements. Because the Bagua and talismans are enigmatic and mysterious, they are not as widely used as Chinese characters.

(1) 八卦與文字
Ba Gua "The Eight Diagrams" and Chinese Characters

159

古人「畫卦結繩，以理海內」。後來，文字代替了結繩，卻代替不了八卦。因為八卦符號象徵自然現象和人事變化，內容包羅萬象，無法用文字來代替。

The ancient Chinese governed the nation by drawing Ba Gua (The Eight Diagrams) and tying knots. Later, written characters replaced the knots but could not replace Ba Gua. This is because the Ba Gua symbols represent natural phenomena and changes in human affairs, encompassing a vast range of meanings that cannot be fully captured by written language.

八卦 The Ba Gua

160

《易經》是一部用八卦來占卜萬物變化的最古老的經典。八卦早於文字，八卦符號並不是文字。

The *I Ching*（Yijing）is the oldest classic used for divination regarding the changes of all things through the Ba Gua（The Eight Diagrams）. The Ba Gua predates written language, and the Ba Gua symbols are not considered written characters.

— —陰爻和——陽爻是構成八卦的基本符號。陰陽是中國古代哲學的一對範疇，是指自然界兩種對立和互相消長的物質勢力。

— — Yin Yao and —— Yang Yao are fundamental symbols that make up the Ba Gua. Yin and Yang are a pair of concepts in ancient Chinese philosophy that refer to two opposing yet interdependent forces in the natural world. They represent the dynamic interplay of contrasting elements, signifying how these forces complement and counterbalance each other, leading to the ongoing cycles of change in nature.

161

八卦（單卦）

Ba Hua, The Eight Diagrams（single hexagram）

☰	乾卦（qián guà, ㄑㄧㄢˊㄍㄨㄚˋ）代表天 Qian Diagram, denoting the heaven
☷	坤卦（kūn guà, ㄎㄨㄣ ㄍㄨㄚˋ）代表地 Kun Diagram, denoting the earth
☳	震卦（zhèn guà, ㄓㄣˋ ㄍㄨㄚˋ）代表雷 Zhen Diagram, denoting thunder
☴	巽卦（xùn guà, ㄒㄩㄣˋ ㄍㄨㄚˋ）代表風 Xun Diagram, denoting wind
☵	坎卦（Kǎn Guà, ㄎㄢˇ ㄍㄨㄚˋ）代表水 Kan Diagram, denoting water
☲	離卦（lí guà , ㄌㄧˊㄍㄨㄚˋ）代表火 Li Diagram, denoting fire
☶	艮卦（gèn guà, ㄍㄣˋ ㄍㄨㄚˋ）代表山 Gen Diagram, denoting mountain
☱	兑卦（duì guà, ㄉㄨㄟˋ ㄍㄨㄚˋ）代表澤 Dui Diagram, denoting swamp

162

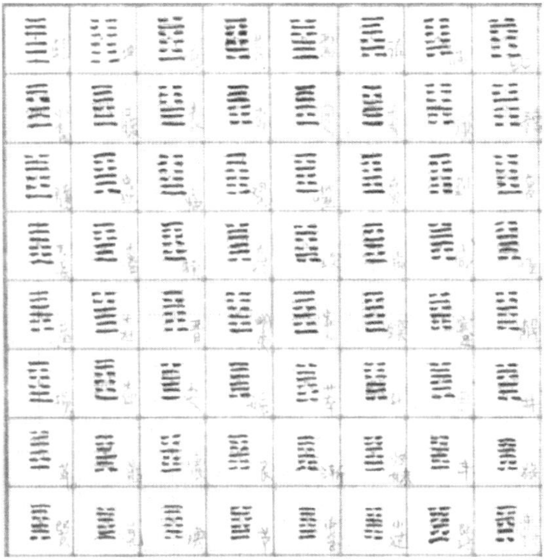

六十四複卦圖

The 64 double hexagrams chart

由八個單卦組合六十四個複卦圖。算命先生以此預測人的命運和各種事情的未來。

The 64 hexagrams are formed by combining the eight basic diagrams. Fortune tellers use these hexagrams to predict a person's destiny and various future events. Each hexagram has its unique interpretation, reflecting different situations and changes in life, and is used as a tool for divination and guidance.

163

傳説，伏羲創制八卦。

According to legend, Fu Xi is credited with the creation of the Ba Gua.

伏羲，神話中的人類始祖，他與他的妹妹女媧結合而生人類。

Fu Xi is the mythical ancestor of humanity in Chinese history, the mythical ancestor of humanity. He is said to have united with his sister, Nu Wa, to give birth to humanity.

伏羲與女媧結合

The union of Fu Xi and Nu Wa

(2) 符籙與文字 Fu Lu "The Taoist Magic Figures" and Chinese Characters

164

各種鎮煞神符

The Taoist Magic Figures

道家符籙是中國的一種民俗文化。

道家符籙是一種筆劃屈曲，似字非字的符號。道士用符籙與神鬼交流，用來轉達神的旨意，召神劾鬼，降妖鎮魔。

Fu Lu（The Taoist Magic Figures）are an aspect of Chinese folk culture.

These symbols consist of twisted and curved strokes, resembling characters but not actual words. Taoist priests use these figures to communicate with spirits and deities, conveying divine intentions, summoning spirits, expelling ghosts, subduing demons, and warding off evil.

鎮宅淨水神符

A Taoist Magic Figure for house-guarding and purification

百解消災符

A Taoist Magic Figure for warding off misfortunes

165

道教是漢族固有的宗教，淵源於古代巫術。道教始於東漢（西元 142 年）時期。

Taoism is an indigenous religion of the Han Chinese, with roots in ancient shamanistic practices. Taoism formally began during the Eastern Han Dynasty around 142 AD.

二十五 影響漢字的歷史人物
Historical Figures who influenced Chinese Characters

166

漢字的創造和發展是中華民族的集體智慧的結晶，影響漢字的歷史人物只是各個事件中的代表。

The creation and development of Chinese characters are the result of the collective wisdom of the Chinese people, with influential historical figures serving as representatives of key events in this ongoing process.

167

倉頡（**cāngjié,** ㄘㄤ ㄒㄧㄝˊ）（遠古時期）

Cang Jie（the ancient times）

倉頡造字

Cang Jie, the inventor of Chinese characters.

傳說，倉頡天生兩對眼睛，觀察力超人。

According to legend, Cang Jie was born with two pairs of eyes and had extraordinary powers of observation.

「昔者倉頡作書而天雨粟，鬼夜哭」。漢字的產生使人類從野蠻走向文明，是驚天動地變化，造化不能藏其密，故天雨粟，靈怪不能遁其形，故鬼夜哭。

In ancient times, when Cang Jie created writing, the heavens rained millet, and ghosts wept at night. The creation of Chinese characters marked humanity's transition from barbarism to civilization, a world-shaking transformation. Nature could not conceal its secrets, hence the rain of millet from the heavens; supernatural beings could not hide their forms, hence the weeping of ghosts at night.

168

秦始皇 qín shǐ huáng（ㄑㄧㄣˊ ㄕˇ ㄏㄨㄤˊ）

（西元前 259-210 年）統一文字

Qin Shi Huang（259-210 B.C.）, who unified Chinese characters

秦始皇在西元前 221 年統一中國後，開始統一文字。

Qin Shi Huang began the process of standardizing Chinese characters, after unifying China in 221 BC.

169

李斯（lǐ sī, ㄌㄧˇ ㄙ）（生年不詳，卒於西元前 208）

Li Si（birth year unknown, died in 208 BC）

秦朝宰相李斯奉秦始皇之命，以秦國的文字為本，制定了全國統一的文字「秦篆」亦稱「小篆」。

Li Si, the prime minister of the Qin Dynasty, was ordered by Qin Shi Huang to use 秦篆（qín zhuàn ㄑㄧㄣˊ ㄓㄨㄢˋ）, the script of the Qin state, as the basis for creating a standardized national script known as "Qin Seal Script", also called 小篆（xiǎo zhuàn ㄑㄧㄣˊㄓㄨㄢˋ）"Small Seal Script".

170

程邈（chéng miǎo, ㄔㄥˊㄇㄧㄠˇ）（生卒年不詳）

Cheng Miao（birth and death years unknown）

程邈創隸書。

程邈因得罪秦始皇而入獄，在獄中他收集和整理了隸書。後來得到秦始皇賞識，任他為御史。

Cheng Miao created Clerical scripts.

Cheng Miao was imprisoned for offending Qin Shi Huang. While in prison, he collected and organized Clerical Script. Later, he gained Qin Shi Huang's favor and was appointed as an imperial historian.

171

許慎（xǔshèn, ㄒㄩˇㄕㄣˋ）（約西元 58 至 147）

Xu Shen（approximately 58 – 147 AD.）

許慎著《說文解字》。

許慎是漢代文字學家，著史上第一部內容完整的漢字字典《說文解字》。字典所錄是當時的小篆。

Xu Shen compiled《說文解字》(shuō wén jiě zì, ㄕㄨㄛ ㄨㄣˊㄐㄧㄝˇㄐㄧㄗˋ), *The Analytical Dictionary of Characters.*

Xu Shen（approximately 58 – 147 AD）was a Chinese philologist of Han Dynasty and author of the first comprehensive Chinese dictionary《說文解字》(shuō wén jiě zì, ㄕㄨㄛ ㄨㄣˊㄐㄧㄝˇㄐㄧ ㄗˋ), *The Analytical Dictionary of Characters.* The dictionary recorded characters in the Small Seal script of that time period.

172

徐鉉（xǔ xuǎn, ㄒㄩˇ ㄒㄩㄢˇ）（西元 916-991）

Xu Xuan（916– 991 AD）

雖然反切注音法產生在東漢（西元前 106 年），但是到了北宋，徐鉉比較系統地校訂了《說文解字》，在每個字之下加入反切注音，使之規範化，成為後來漢語注音、拼音的模式。

Although the Fanqie phonetic method originated in the Eastern Han Dynasty（106 BC）, it was during the Northern Song Dynasty that Xu Xuan systematically revised《說文解字》(shuō wén jiě zì, ㄕㄨㄛ ㄨㄣˊㄐㄧㄝˇ ㄐㄧ ㄗˋ）, *The Analytical Dictionary of Characters*. He added fanqie phonetic annotations under each character, standardizing it and laying the foundation for later Chinese phonetic notation and Pinyin systems.

173

康熙（kāng xī, ㄎㄤ ㄒㄧ）（西元 1654 – 1722）

Kang Xi（1654 – 1722 AD）

清代皇帝康熙於西元 1710 年下令編寫《康熙字典》。這部字典共收集了 47035 個正體字，是 18 世紀和 19 世紀標準的漢字字典。

Emperor Kangxi of the Qing Dynasty ordered the compilation of the *Kangxi Dictionary* in 1710. This dictionary collected a total of 47,035 traditional characters and became the standard Chinese dictionary of the 18th and 19th centuries.

174

（Image credit: WIKIMEDIA COMMONS）

王懿榮（Wáng Yì Róng, ㄨㄤˊ ㄧˋ ㄖㄨㄥˊ）（西元 1845 – 1900）

Wang Yi Rong（1845 – 1900 AD）

王懿榮因發現甲骨文，被稱為甲骨文之父。

Wang Yi Rong is known as the “Father of Oracle Bone Script” for his discovery of oracle bone inscriptions.

清朝光緒年間（19 世紀末）國子監王懿榮偶然一次在中藥材中發現甲骨文，使甲骨文重見天日。

During the Guangxu era of the Qing Dynasty（late 19th century）, Wang Yi Rong（1845–1900）, the head scholar of the Imperial Academy, accidentally discovered oracle bone inscriptions among traditional Chinese medicinal materials, bringing the Oracle Bone script back to light.

175

（Image credit: Wikipedia）

英國人威妥瑪（1818 -1895 年）

British scholar Sir Thomas Francis Wade（1818-1895）

（Image credit: Wikipedia）

英國人翟理斯（1845-1935 年）。

British scholar Sir Herbert Allen Giles（1845-1935）

威妥瑪和翟理斯都是駐華的英國外交家和漢學家。由威妥瑪創造，後來翟理斯修改而成的一套用於漢語的羅馬拼音系統，即威翟式拼音，曾經成為中文的標準英譯拼音，也為後來國語注音符號和拼音字母的制定提供了參考。

Thomas Francis Wade and Herbert Allen Giles were both British diplomats and sinologists stationed in China. The Romanization system for Chinese phonetic notation created by Wade and later modified by Giles, known as the Wade-Giles system, once became the standard Romanization for Chinese phonetics. It also served as a reference for the development of the Mandarin Phonetic Symbols and the Pinyin system.

二十六 漢字文化圈

The Chinese Character Cultural Sphere

176

歷史上，漢字曾被交趾（部分交趾今為越南）、高麗（今南、北朝鮮）和日本等亞洲國家借用，因而形成了漢字文化圈。

Historically, Chinese characters were borrowed by Asian countries such as Jiaozhi（part of which is now Vietnam）, Goryeo（present-day North and South Korea）, and Japan, thereby forming the Chinese Character Cultural Sphere.

177

西漢（西元前 202-8 年）末年，漢字傳至交趾（部分交趾今為越南）。到西元 13 世紀，越南人以漢字為素材，創造了喃字，例如「𡨸」，讀音 chu，「字」的意思。越南現代的「國語字」的拉丁字母拼寫是在 17 世紀由法國傳教士 Alexandre de Rhodes 整合完成的。「國語字」在 19 世紀流行，20 世紀全面使用。1945 年越南完全放棄漢字。

In the late Western Han Dynasty（202 BC - 8 AD）,

Chinese characters were introduced to Jiaozhi（part of which is now Vietnam）. By the 13th century, the Vietnamese created the Chu Nom script using Chinese characters as the foundation. For example, the Chu Nom character 𡨸（pronounced “chu”）means 字, “character”. The modern Latin alphabet spelling of Chu Quoc Ngu was integrated in the 17th century by French missionary Alexandre de Rhodes. Chu Quoc Ngu became popular in the 19th century and was fully adopted in the 20th century. In 1945, Vietnam completely abandoned Chinese characters.

178

西元 3 世紀左右，漢字傳入高麗（今朝鮮和韓國）。1446 年高麗正式使用自己創造的字母拼寫諺文。1948 年韓國決定放棄漢字，但是大多數的人名和地名還使用漢字。

Around the 3rd century AD, Chinese characters were introduced to Goryeo（present-day Korea）. In 1446, Goryeo officially adopted its own created script, known as Hangul. In 1948, South Korea decided to abandon Chinese characters; however, most personal names and place names still use Chinese characters.

paddy field

畓 = 水 + 田，「水田」的意思，是一個會意字。畓是韓造漢字，韓語唸 da bo.

畓（da bo）“paddy field”, is a Korean-made Chinese character.

畓 = 水 “water” + 田 “field” combine to mean “paddy field”, and is a Joint Ideogram character. 畓 is a Korean-created Chinese character and is pronounced “da bo” in Korean.

179

西元 5 世紀左右，漢字傳入日本。借來的漢字、和制漢字、加上日本自製的平假名和片假名組成了日本文字。

Around the 5th century AD, Chinese characters（Kanji）were introduced to Japan. The borrowed Chinese characters, Japanese-made Kanji, along with the Japanese-created Hiragana and Katakana, formed the Japanese writing system.

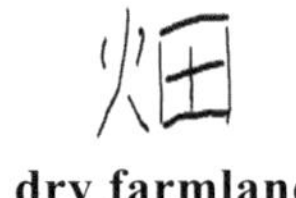

dry farmland

畑 = 火 + 田，「旱田」的意思，是一個會意字。畑是和制漢字，日語唸はた Ha-Ta。

畑（はた hata）, “dry farmland”, is a Japan-made Kanji. 畑 = 火 fire + 田 field, and is a Joint Ideogram character. It is pronounced “hata” in Japanese.

180

越南、高麗、日本的歷史學家必須精通漢字，才能閱讀他們的古典書籍。

Historians in Vietnam, Korea, and Japan must be proficient in Chinese characters to read their classical texts.

181

漢字的命運與中華民族的興衰緊密地聯結在一起。

The destiny of Chinese characters is closely linked to the rise and fall of the Chinese nation.

西安阿倍仲麻呂紀念碑

Monument of Abe no Nakamaro in Xi An, built in February 1979

唐代（628-907 年），中國是世界上最富有、最多人口、最文明的國家。其文化深刻地影響了整個亞洲。許多外國留學生到中國來學習文化。阿倍仲麻呂あべのなかまろ是最為出色的日本留學生，他取名晁衡，在他十六歲那年由日本政府派往中國學習，後來他高中進士，成為唐代著名的政治家和詩人。當時日本的上層社會紛紛仿效中國人，只有懂得書寫漢字才算是有教養的人。

During the Tang Dynasty（618-907）, China was the richest, most populous, and most civilized country in the world. Its culture profoundly influenced other Asian countries, and many international students came to China to study its culture. Abe no Nakamaro（あべのなかまろ）was the most outstanding Japanese student; he took the name Chao Heng（晁衡）. At sixteen, he was sent by the Japanese government to study in China, where he later passed the imperial examination and became a renowned politician and poet of the Tang Dynasty. At that time, the Japanese upper class imitated the Chinese, and only those who could write Chinese characters were considered cultured.

在十九世紀中葉，中國的洋務運動和日本的明治維新幾乎同時開展，它們都是提倡學習西方文明的社會改革，其結果是中國半途而廢，反而日本全面西化。日本提倡翻譯外國著作，他們創製了大量的現代常用的漢語詞彙，例如，資本主義、理論、封建、共和、政治、經濟、證券、儲蓄、方針、政策、革命、黨、機關、部門、後勤、會議、哲學、科學、創作、發明、美學、美術、衛生、總理、法人、幹部、代表、邏輯、抽象、印象、申請、原則、規則、概念、系統、反對、解決、克服、刺激、勞動、健康、細胞、參觀、服務……等等。

In the mid-19th century, China's Westernization Movement and Japan's Meiji Restoration unfolded almost simultaneously; both were social reforms advocating for learning from Western civilization. However, while China's effort ended halfway, Japan fully embraced Westernization. Japan promoted the translation of foreign works and created a substantial amount of modern, commonly used Chinese vocabulary, including words such as capitalism（資本主義）, theory（理論）, feudalism（封建）, republic（共和）, politics（政治）, economy（經濟）, securities（證券）, savings（儲蓄）, policy（方針）, policy（政策），revolution（革命）, party（黨）, institution（機關）, department（部門）, logistics（後勤）, conference（會議）, philosophy（哲學）, science（科學）, creation（創作）, invention（發明）, aesthetics（美學）, art（美術）, hygiene（衛生）, premier（總理）, juridical person（法人）, cadre（幹部）, representative（代表）, logic（邏輯）, abstract（抽象）, impression（印象）, application（申請）, principle（原則）, rule（規則）, concept（概念）, system（系統）, oppose（反對）, solve（解決）, overcome（克服）, stimulate（刺激）, labor（勞動）, health（健康）, cell（細胞）, visit（參觀）, service（服務）, and many others.

182

甲午戰爭（1894 年）之後，大清加速衰亡。日本要廢除漢字，但是可笑的是，日本在報紙上發表那份去除漢字的聲明用的是漢字。日本始終擺脱不了漢字。

After the First Sino-Japanese War（1894）, the decline of the Qing Dynasty accelerated. Japan sought to abolish Chinese characters; however, it is ironic that the statement to eliminate Chinese characters published in Japanese newspapers was written using Chinese characters（Kanji）. Japan has never been able to fully escape the influence of Chinese characters.

1946 年日本政府發表了規定使用 1850 個漢字的《當用漢字表》。這 1850 個之外的漢字不再使用，大量地減少使用漢字，而增加假名的使用。

In 1946, the Japanese government issued the "List of Kanji for Common Use", which specified the use of 1,850 Chinese characters. Characters outside of these 1,850 were no longer used, significantly reducing the use of Chinese characters while increasing the use of Kana（the Japanese syllabary）.

但是，今天漢字仍然是日本文化中的正式和莊重的象徵。在日本的正式場合和重大事件中的書寫都是使用漢字。

However, today, Chinese characters still serve as a symbol of formality and solemnity in Japanese culture. Writing in formal occasions and significant events in Japan is done using Chinese characters.

從 1995 年起，日本漢字能力檢定協會每年向全國徵集一個「今年の漢字」，在年終時公佈，以表現該年世態和國民的感受。例如，2019 年的「今年の漢字」是「令」字，標記該年是令和元年，也代表了國民關注該年的「法令改正」。由此可見，漢字在日本的重要地位。

Since 1995, the Japan Kanji Aptitude Test Association has annually collected a “Kanji of the Year” from across the country, announcing it at the end of the year to reflect the social climate and the sentiments of the people. For example, the “Kanji of the Year” for 2019 was “令”（rei）, marking it as the first year of the Reiwa era and reflecting the public’s attention to that year’s 法令改正, “legal revisions”. This illustrates the significant status of Chinese characters in Japan.

183

第二次世界大戰後，除了新加坡（華人佔四分之三的新加坡總人口）之外的其他東南亞國家都放棄漢字，關閉華文學校。印尼最為嚴厲，在上世紀60年代立法禁止人名、公司名、店名和其他任何名稱使用漢字，關閉了全國所有的華文學校，在此後的30多年裡無華文學校，迫使成千上萬的華僑子女寧願放棄國籍，回到中國學習華語。當時中國正處在經濟困難時期，但是中國政府仍然派船前往印尼，先後接回數以萬計的青少年學生，讓他們免費繼續完成學業。

After World War II, all Southeast Asian countries, except for Singapore（where Chinese people constitute three-quarters of the total population）, abandoned Chinese characters and closed Chinese language schools. Indonesia was the most stringent, enacting legislation in the 1960s that prohibited the use of Chinese characters in personal names, company names, shop names, and any other names, resulting in the closure of all Chinese language schools across the country. For over three decades, there were no Chinese language schools, forcing thousands of Chinese expatriate children to give up their nationality and return to China to learn Chinese. At that time, China was experiencing economic difficulties; however, the Chinese government still sent ships to Indonesia and brought back tens of thousands of young students, allowing them to continue their education for free.

184

20 世紀 70 年代中國的改革開放使國家再度復興，漢字在漢字文化圈的國家中再度復活，勢如「野火燒不盡，春風吹又生」。

The "Reform and Opening-up" policy in China during the 1970s revitalized the country, leading to a resurgence of Chinese characters in nations within the Chinese character cultural sphere. This phenomenon is akin to the saying, "Wildfires cannot consume it all; the spring breeze brings it back to life".

185

現今中國的經濟發展影響全球，漢字文化圈中的國家都解禁了漢字，允許學校開設漢語班，鼓勵學生學習漢字。在許多外國的車站、機場等公共場所都可以看到漢字的指示牌。

Today, China's economic development has a global impact, leading to the lifting of restrictions on Chinese characters in countries within the Chinese character cultural sphere. These nations now allow schools to offer Chinese language classes and encourage students to learn Chinese characters. In many foreign train stations, airports, and other public places, signs featuring Chinese characters can be seen, reflecting the increasing recognition and integration of Chinese culture worldwide.

二十七 永不消逝的古老文字

The Everlasting Ancient Characters

186

當我們將一些甲骨文與蘇美爾楔形文字和埃及聖書字比較時，就會驚訝地發現，它們竟然如此雷同。這是象形文字超時空的邂逅。

When we compare some Chinese oracle bone inscriptions with Sumerian cuneiform and Egyptian hieroglyphs, we are surprised to find that they bear remarkable similarities. This represents an extraordinary convergence of pictographic writing across different times and spaces.

187

甲骨文和蘇美爾楔形文字比較

Comparison between Chinese oracle bone scripts and the ancient Sumerian cuneiform

甲骨文 商代 （西元前 16-11 世紀） Chinese oracle bone scripts Shang Dynasty （16th to 11th centuries BC）	蘇美爾楔形文字 兩河流域文明時代 （約西元前 3000 年左右） The ancient Sumerian cuneiform The era of Mesopotamia civilization（3000 BC）	字義 Character meaning
		水（shuǐ, ㄕㄨㄟˇ） water
		魚（yú, ㄩˊ） fish
		足（zú, ㄗㄨˊ） foot

188

甲骨文和埃及聖書字比較

Comparison between Chinese Oracle Bone scripts and the ancient Egyptian hieroglyphs

甲骨文 商代 （西元前 16-11 世紀） Chinese oracle bone scripts Shang Dynasty （16th to 11th centuries BC）	埃及聖書字 埃及第一王朝 （約西元前 2100） The ancient Egyptian hieroglyphs First Dynasty of Egypt （2100 BC）	字義 Character meaning
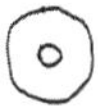	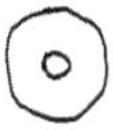	日（rì, ㄖˋ） sun
		山（shān, ㄕㄢ） mountain
		鳥（niǎo, ㄋㄧ ㄠ）ˇ bird

189

中國漢字、古埃及聖書字、古巴比倫楔形文字和古瑪雅文字是世界四大最古老的象形文字。至今只有中國漢字存活，其他文字已經消逝了數千年。因此，漢字是人類象形文字的活化石，是世界共同的文化遺產。

Chinese characters, ancient Egyptian hieroglyphs, ancient Babylonian cuneiform, and ancient Mayan script are regarded as the four oldest pictographic writing systems in the world. To this day, only Chinese characters have survived, while the others have disappeared for thousands of years. Therefore, Chinese characters serve as a living fossil of human pictographic writing and represent a shared cultural heritage of the world.

本書引用
References

《説文解字》，許慎，中華書局出版

《康熙字典》，引之校改本，上海古籍出版社

《漢字的文化史》，藤枝晃（日本）

《當前文字改革的任務》，周恩來，1958 年 1 月 10 日在政協全國委員會舉行的報告會上的報告

《現代漢語詞典》（試用本），中國科學院語言研究所詞典編輯室編，商務印書館

《漢英大辭典》，上海交通大學出版社

廣雅指南 02

漢字簡説

作　　者：邢福雷 著　邢荃 修訂
書面題字：莫海濤
內文插圖：邢福雷
責任編輯：黎漢傑
設計排版：陳先英
法律顧問：陳煦堂 律師

出　　版：初文出版社有限公司
電郵：manuscriptpublish@gmail.com

印　　刷：陽光印刷製本廠

發　　行：香港聯合書刊物流有限公司
香港新界荃灣德士古道220-248號
荃灣工業中心16樓
電話：(852) 2150-2100　傳真：(852) 2407-3062

海外總經銷：貿騰發賣股份有限公司
電話：886-2-82275988　傳真：886-2-82275989
網址：www.namode.com

版　　次：2024年6月初版
國際書號：978-988-71098-2-2
定　　價：港幣98元　新臺幣360元

Published and printed in Hong Kong

香港印刷及出版